by
Christopher Carr
and illustrated by Matthew Jeffery

HENDERSON
PUBLISHING PLC
©1996 HENDERSON PUBLISHING PLC

Chapter 1

Sam Procter stopped the car, turned off the engine and checked his map again. There were no other cars on the road, and there hadn't been any for the last few miles. The way ahead was silent, and they might have been a million miles from nowhere. Alison took the opportunity to stretch her legs and jumped out.

"Lost *again,* dad?" she smirked.

"Here, let me out too, I'm starting to feel like a parcel," cried Tim, her younger brother.

Tim hadn't stopped complaining about sitting in the back since their last stop. That had been two and a half hours earlier. The small car was stuffed full of their belongings, and Tim shared the back seat with several holdalls and piles of sleeping bags.

Alison crouched down, then pointed her toes, repeating the 'warm-up' exercises she had been shown at school. Tim watched her for a moment, then pulled a face and laughed. Across the road was the promise of a view, beyond a low moss-green wall. He went to gaze across the valley.

Tim whistled, as he stared at the empty silence of the place.

"It's a long way down!" he called back to his father.

Sam Procter was twisting his road map, one way and then the other. Suddenly, he let out a cry of victory.

"No, it's OK. I was right. This is just down the alternative road, we're on the right track. It shouldn't be far now."

He tossed the map onto the passenger seat and joined his children. Alison now stood beside her brother, and stared across the patchy black stone hillside.

"It's peculiar, isn't it?" she said.

"What do you mean?" her father asked. "I think it's a great view."

"Sure, but it's kind of bleak, all those greys and dark colours. It's as though somebody had pulled a veil over the place."

Sam Procter cocked his head to one side and considered her comment for a moment.

"It's just a view," said Tim. "That's all."

Sam screwed up his eyes and peered beyond the ribbon of forest, which ran along the valley floor. Further down from the trees, a mottled patchwork of brown and slate grey roofs stood proud against the hillside.

"See there," Sam said, pointing beyond the forest. "I may be wrong, it's difficult to tell from here, but I believe that's Lofton."

The children were unimpressed. The view *was* great, but Alison did have a point. It was a country scene, but a country scene with a definite kind of atmosphere.

"So," said Alison, "our place must be somewhere in that forest?"

"Forest?" sniffed Tim. "You mean that

clump of trees?"

His father ruffled his son's hair. Tim hated that, it made him feel like a very small boy.

"Misery guts," said Sam. "Yes. That's the place. The forest is called Martyn's Close, and somewhere at the edge of that - *forest*," he glared at his son with emphasis, "is what will be the finest restaurant in the Pennines."

"Martyn's Close, eh?" Alison whispered the name. They stood in silence for a moment, just taking it all in.

Beyond the forest, leading out of the valley, came a sudden shaft of amber sunshine. The place shimmered like a desert mirage. It was as though the sun had just been turned down a notch, and the effect was startling. The landscape glowed with a strange sombre light. Colours changed, becoming a muted sheen. Shadows fell like a criss-cross webbing. A spell might have suddenly been cast. It was a place at the edge of a dream.

Despite the warmth of the late afternoon, Alison shivered. The view betrayed a sense of unease - pretty enough on the outside but concealing a secret too dreadful to tell. She shivered once more.

Alison wondered why.

The turning off the main road had arrived as a surprise. Driving through a broken farm gate, the car took a dirt track fork to the left. A cavern of trees reached above them; snatches of light speckled the road ahead like a ballroom glitter ball.

"The road's a bit bumpy here," said Sam. "I've asked the builders to come up with a plan for another access."

"And you'll need a sign," said Tim.

"A big board with the name of our restaurant on it!" Alison stretched her arms to demonstrate a possible size, her eyes sparkled.

Their father half-smiled, "Bigger than that I think."

"Hey," said Alison suddenly. "Just what are you going to call the restaurant? How about Procter's Place?"

"Mm, Procter's Place? I don't know, it sounds a bit American, a bit touristy."

"What about plain and simple: Meat and Two Veg?" suggested Tim.

Sam Procter snorted. "No, certainly not. We're going to be very up-market, a special place. As I told you, it's an old mill. It's *very* old. I mean, we're talking about hundreds of years."

"Mum told us that there were parts that date back to Medieval times." said Alison. "Maybe even earlier?"

"That's possibly true," he grinned proudly. "That's going to be part of the character, the attraction. It's had bits and pieces built on over the years, you know how it is. It's known as Martyn's Mille locally. That's mill with an e on the end. I want to keep the old spelling, and I want to keep the name."

"Martyn's Mille," Tim considered this for a moment. He thought it sounded odd.

"Who was Martyn?" asked Alison.

Before her father could reply, from out of a side turning ahead, came a white van. Sam swerved the car to the left; the van held the middle of the path.

"He's heading straight for us!" yelled Tim.

Sam honked the horn. The van kept coming with a frightening urgency. Sam weaved and pulled the car over to the left. The van sped on past.

"Idiot!" screamed Alison.

Her father crashed the gears as he started off again.

"I may be wrong, but I think that was one of our builders," said Sam quietly, "they all seem to use those white vans. What did he think he was playing at?"

"But did you see the look on his face?" Tim remarked.

Alison turned round and frowned at her brother.

"What do you mean?"

"Well, I only caught a quick look at him, but whoever he was, he looked terrified."

Sam Procter glanced over his shoulder, but said nothing. He replayed the scene in his head. Perhaps his son was right.

They took the turning just ahead of where the car had emerged. Alison's eyes widened. It was as though they had driven into a secret glade - a wonderland. The newly cut stubs of tree branches revealed that this part of the forest had recently been cleared. Through what seemed like an archway of green, stood the brown cobbled building. They had arrived at Martyn's Mille.

Alison's first thoughts was that it was like a miniature medieval castle. The small busy river even ran into a miniature moat to the left, and there was a bridge too.

A large cream coloured sign had been pinned to a nearby tree. It read: "Martyn's Mille. Development work by W. Smollett - Builders, Ltd, Lofton. Completion, Christmas Eve."

Concrete mixers stood like lonely sentries, and piles of timber, heaped into neatly arranged stacks, were everywhere. Two white vans, similar to the one that had sped past them, were parked to the left of a small cabin outbuilding.

Sam pulled the car over and parked. The children were anxious to get out.

"That's strange," said Sam.

"What's wrong, dad?" Tim asked.

Alison had run ahead. She stood in front of the mill and gazed upwards, gradually taking in the sturdy turret-like shape of the building.

"Hallo?" called Sam. "Where is everybody?"

Suddenly, a figure appeared in the doorway of the cabin. He was obviously one of the builders, dressed in a pair of brown overalls and a carpenter's apron. The cabin was the builder's makeshift canteen.

"Dad," said Tim, nudging his father. "Over there."

Sam Procter's face lit up.

"That's the contractor's foreman, his name's Geoff. He's OK. I wonder what's going on."

Together, they walked across to the cabin. But as they approached the door, they heard a sudden cry from inside. It was the voice of a man, and he sounded distressed.

"Geoff," said Sam with a nod, trying to crane his neck to see within.

The foreman touched his cap, then he held his face in his hands and gave a deep sigh.

"You best come in," he said.

Sam tried again to see past him, there was some kind of commotion going on in the corner. Clearly there were problems.

Outside, Alison rushed on to the bridge and gazed down at the clear water beneath. Feathery lines of foam and strands of reed were tossed against the banks.

She looked up and craned her neck. Past the

main turret of the building was a courtyard, and a huge mill wheel. This place was her father's dream, come true at last, and she could see why. It looked as good as he had described, and they would be spending the whole summer here, helping and preparing for the 'big move'.

The busy cries of men's voices made her look over her shoulder. Her father and brother stood beside the door of the cabin. Two men were helping a third out between them. The middle man looked as though he could hardly stand, and his face was crumpled into creases of dismay. He alternately mumbled, then broke into small cries. At one point he shook his head and gave way to more sobs. Somebody drove one of the vans to where they stood.

Alison promptly crossed back to the bank and hurried over. She was met half way by her brother. Tim looked pale.

"What, what on earth's wrong?" she asked. "Is he ill?"

She looked over Tim's shoulder: the man was being helped into the van, and her father was talking to the foreman.

"Tim?" she urged. "What's the matter?"

"I'm not sure," replied her brother.

"But why is he like that? Is he hurt?"

Tim looked back at his father, catching his eye. He remembered the face of the driver who had passed them on the road.

"He's one of the workmen. The man was working in a room at the rear of the mill.

FEAR OF THE DARK

Something happened, then he slipped, he said something about the darkness - I don't know what he meant. He's had a slight accident with a drill."

"A slight accident with a drill?"

Alison glanced back at the figure in the van who was holding his bandaged hand, and became aware of the sudden solid silence of the rest of the men around them.

She didn't believe them.

"Workmen don't behave like this when they have minor accidents." Her thought pierced the weight of the silence.

Even the birds had stopped singing. Then she looked into the foreman's face.

Something *had* happened here. Something more than an accident with a power drill.

Chapter 2

"Jim Harris just got a bit careless, that's all," Smollett began. "We've been having some sort of problem with the electrics here. Lamps blowing and such, we've gone through boxes of light bulbs like they've been going out of fashion. He was working in a difficult spot with a safety lamp. It blew - and he just got a touch of the frights in the dark."

Sam Procter watched Smollett, who paced up and down the cabin floor like an animal in a cage. Somehow he was trying too hard.

"Jim's been having problems at home as well. He says he can't sleep properly since he started on the job here. You know how it is. I expect being plunged into darkness just shook him up a bit."

Alison watched from the doorway. That Bill Smollett was concerned. He was a chunky, red-faced man, with short white hair, whose head was hunched into his shoulders. His face was furrowed with worry lines and he had an anxious, haunted look about him with deep brown nicotine stains on his fingers. He was a strange partner beside her father, who was gaunt and thin, almost like a matchstick man.

Smollett had arrived within minutes of the foreman driving Jim Harris home. What puzzled Alison the most was, that beneath his bravado of excuses, he seemed genuinely worried. She re-ran the scene in her mind, and remembered the faces of the workmen again. Excuses were coming too easily.

"Look, Sam," Smollett paused and swallowed. "There's a few further things to report - on the progress, like." He glanced in Alison's direction. Until then he seemed not to have noticed her. Smollett gestured with his head that she should leave, then he turned to Alison's father. He ran his fingers through his hair as though embarrassed, and was again searching for the right words.

"Go outside Alison," said Sam, "there's a girl. Mr Smollett needs to talk business with me. Please."

Alison groaned, she had not wanted to miss anything.

"Go and have a wander around. Take a look at the work in the front part of the house, they've made great progress."

Smollett looked up suddenly.

"That's OK, isn't it?" asked her father, aware of his glance.

Smollett swallowed and nodded.

"Aye, no harm."

Alison reluctantly twirled away from the doorway, and out into the remains of the day.

"Don't go in the Wheel House though, not just now," Smollett called after her. She looked back. Then he added, "Not safe yet - but it will be."

His lower lip trembled, ever so slightly.

The light in the forecourt area was fading. Smollett had dismissed his builders shortly after arriving, and now the place was silent. There was not even the rustle of a leaf or the call of a bird.

Tim crouched on the bank beside the bridge. He was watching the river, as his sister had been earlier. It was hypnotic. Even the delicate sounds of the bubbles and froth were muted. He threw pebbles into the water and they landed with a satisfying 'plop'. This seemed to reassure him that they were still in the real world. She went across to him.

"Dad's talking," said Alison. "You know - business."

He didn't seem to hear her. Instead, he looked up into the mosaic ceiling of leaves. Flecks of fading sunset threw dappled shadows around them. The mill had captured him, more so than his sister. The sense of peace and the solitariness had snatched him into its arms.

Alison tried again.

"Dad and that Mr Smollett are pacing the floor like tigers back there."

Tim cracked his knuckles. She hated this. Usually it was a sign that all was not well, that he was on edge. The crunch of dislocated joints echoed into the forest, reminding her of the crack of snapped twigs.

"Tim!" she yelled at him. "You know I don't

like it when you do that, and you're making me nervous."

He looked up, blue eyes peered through his floppy blonde fringe. "Sorry."

"You're drifting off somewhere or other - that's not like you. Dad said we can look inside, come on."

Tim got up and threw the remainder of his pebbles into the stream. Alison went ahead of him, across the bridge to the main turret of the building. The walls shone like gem stones, the builders had cleaned the brick and the stone and flint sections too. Only the crossed masking tape on the windows and the glass panelled entrance betrayed any signs that workmen had been there.

Alison pushed the doors wide open, and waited as her brother caught up with her. For a moment he stood and stared at the entrance.

"Come on," she said. "It's OK."

He hesitated, then stepped forward. Something *was* bothering him.

As the door swung closed, the unexpected smell of newly varnished timber caught their nostrils. The floors were bare board, and a dado rail ran around the walls the height of her shoulder.

· Tim turned and edged his way along the corridor; it was fairly gloomy. Turning right, he entered a large empty room. At the far end was a glass window that almost filled the entire wall. This overlooked the enclosed courtyard.

Beyond, they had a better view of the wheel.

"Dad said that's where the restaurant is going to be," said Tim. "Over there. Beside that square-shaped building - that's the Wheel House."

Tim looked through the window. The huge wheel threw a long oval across the courtyard.

"Look over there," said Alison pointing. "There's still a lot of clearing up to do. Perhaps they've only just started."

Tim followed the direction of her finger. The left hand edge of the courtyard looked even more like a building site than the front.

"So, did you hear what happened exactly?" she asked.

"He was in some room off the Wheel House. I guess it must be round the back there," he looked through the window. For a moment something flashed in the distance like a shard of sudden light. He stepped back and looked through the window again. Perhaps it was his own reflection.

She followed the direction of his stare.

"*So that's the Wheel House then,*" she whispered. Tim turned to face her.

"They really closed up when they saw me, I just heard a little. One man, I think he was called Ray, was huddled in the corner with some others, talking. He said something like '*that's why he wouldn't go in there, not even for double wages.*' Another man was laughing at him, telling him it was all rot. That's, well that's when this other one - the foreman, chipped in."

"Go on," she moved closer.

"He said - 'well how come John Cooper had tore off like a mad thing?' That's what he said, then he noticed me and shut up."

Alison remembered the van that had sped past them.

"The man in the white van?"

Tim shrugged his shoulders. "Could be. I've a feeling this John Cooper was working with him."

She waited for a moment before asking. "Do you think it was the accident with the drill that bothered him, or was it something else?"

He looked up.

Alison walked slowly across the floor, taking equal steps. "This is a great room," she said, changing the subject.

"I think it's to be our living room, or dad mentioned some plan about having it as a small library."

"A library?" she laughed and wrinkled her nose at the thought. Sam Procter liked collecting books but never seemed to read any of them.

Tim continued looking through the window at the Wheel House. A large shadow had fallen across the wall. She watched her brother closely. Since their arrival he had been preoccupied, perhaps he was just tired.

"That builder said we shouldn't go in the Wheel House."

He looked over his shoulder. "Why not?"

"Just, just that it isn't safe or something. Perhaps there's still boards up and all that kind of stuff. Probably no lights."

Alison reached for the light switch and twisted the dimmer control. Nothing happened.

"The electricity can't be connected here either."

Tim pointed at the ceiling, a broken bulb was stuck in the socket. "No light bulbs, that's all."

She laughed. But her amusement lasted moments only. The sound of her footsteps seemed everywhere as she walked back to the doorway. The corridor that led to the front door telescoped away. It was an odd effect, as though it were a trick of the light.

Her father and Bill Smollett stood in the distance, like figures at the end of a tunnel. They had stepped out from the cabin, but her father was waving his hands in the air as if in anger.

Just then, her father seemed to punch the air. This was unlike him, and she frowned. Smollett raised his hands as though warning him to calm down, then turned and headed towards his car in a hurry. Sam Procter looked across at the mill and with determined strides made his way towards them.

"Dad's coming," said Alison. "He looks madder than a gorilla."

Tim joined her and they walked down the corridor to meet their father at the front door. But he had stopped on the bridge and was looking down into the water.

"What's going on? Is something wrong?" asked Alison.

"We've got serious problems," was all he said. "And I wasn't planning on any!"

Chapter 3

The light became thinner surprisingly quickly. Sam Procter had set aside a room further down the corridor. There were camp cot beds, and a few basic sticks of furniture which he had brought out of storage for the holiday visit. For a while he stormed about like a bear with a very sore head, and wished his wife had been able to join them. His eyes glared, and at times the children thought they were even beginning to glow in the dark. But he refused to say anything, and they dared not ask - not yet.

Outside, the approaching evening contributed to the gloom, caused by the tight cover of the trees. Their father continued to trip over bricks and tools, cursing the builders at every stumble.

"I'm sorry," he said finally. "This is ridiculous. Let's get sorted out."

For several minutes he disappeared into a side cupboard beside the main door. Suddenly, the approach to the bridge was lit with floods, thrown there from a series of halogen lights fixed to poles and points on the corners of the buildings.

"That's better," he said, "only temporary - the builders rigged these up." He pushed a box of light bulbs towards Tim.

"There's a small pair of steps in the big room," he went on. "Would you both pop a bulb in the socket in there? They keep blowing. Our Mr Smollett was supposed to have done this for us."

"Come on," said Alison, grabbing her brother by the arm.

"I'm going to be round by the Wheel House," Sam added. "I just want to see what the Lone Ranger and his boys have been doing."

With that he walked briskly to the end of the passage, and threw open the rear door without bothering to close it behind him.

The two children looked at one another.

"The Lone Ranger?" said Tim.

"Cowboys, dumbo. Dad's talking about the builders, he's being deeply ironic. You know what dad can be like sometimes."

"They've upset him, that Mr Smollett's said something, hasn't he?"

"Oh, well done," said Alison, selecting a couple of bulbs from the box. "Observation - ten out of ten. I've a hunch about all this."

"What do you mean?"

Without replying, she led the way back to their room. Beside a partially stripped chest of drawers were a new pair of metal steps. She opened them with a struggle.

"Real imagination, this Mr Smollett," Tim mumbled, "a single light flex bang smack in the middle of the room."

"I bet they're behind with the schedule," said Alison. "That's what dad's all riled about.

"That's my hunch - you can see all of that building stuff unused around the back."

Tim nodded.

"I heard mum and him talking before we left," Alison continued. "Dad's got to open the restaurant at Christmas, otherwise he's in some sort of trouble with the bank."

Suddenly, from somewhere outside, came the noise of a car horn - a series of tones, as if its driver was expected.

"Who's that?" asked Alison.

"Only one way to find out," said Tim, putting the box of light bulbs on top of the chest of drawers.

Alison was ahead of him, and ran down the corridor to the bridge. Back across the yard, just discernible within the cover of the trees, were a pair of dull flickering headlights. Alison crossed the bridge and stood beneath the rays of the halogens. A large, dark coloured van, which at first she thought was an ice-cream van, tumbled through the trees, and pulled to a halt in the forecourt with a squeal of brakes.

The head lamps dimmed, and almost as suddenly a light went on within the van. Alison could hardly believe her eyes - it *was* an ice-cream van, or something similar. She turned to her brother, who had arrived behind her.

"I don't believe this. Want a flake, Tim?" she giggled.

A large bear of a man with a grubby white apron and a big bushy black beard, sloped out of the driver's seat. He was joined from the passenger side by a small girl in a similar apron who wore a baseball cap the wrong way round.

"You must be Mr Procter's kids?" he said.

"Yeah, I'm Alison, this is Tim."

The man returned a casual smile, and gestured back at the van.

"Flake, you said? Can't do that. I can probably do better, though."

Tim rushed forward to the side of the van, the shutter had been secured above the window opening. He raised his nose and sniffed the air.

"Vinegar! Salt and vinegar!"

"Fish and chips." Alison's smile widened like a crocodile's.

"The best in the area," said the small girl in a matter-of-fact voice. "Will that be cod or plaice?"

The man climbed into the back of the van and threw back several chrome lids. Steam billowed out through the window. The small girl shuffled a basin of chips with a wire basket. Within moments the sizzle and smell was like 'deep fry' heaven.

"Who's there?" called a voice.

In the distance Sam Procter appeared at the bridge, he flashed a torch at them.

"Fish and chips, dad!"

The man with the beard leant out of the window.

"Sam Procter? Hi there. I'm Bob Walters, this is my daughter Kelly. Didn't think you'd mind us making a detour here."

Sam Procter smacked the side of his head with his palm. He realised that his kids hadn't eaten anything but sandwiches all day. He switched off the flashlight he had been carrying, and crossed the forecourt. He shook Bob Walter's hand.

"So my name doesn't ring a bell then?"

"Wait a minute. . . Walters, Bill's foreman is *Geoff* Walters."

"That's the one," said Bob Walters. "My brother. I gather you're going to be competition to my Fish and Chip circuit eventually. The mill is almost on my round. He called me up and suggested that we dropped in on you. He thought you might want something, even cheering up."

They sat together beneath the floodlights, making little conversation, but satisfying their appetites. Bob Walters handed Sam a cup of steaming tea.

"Bit stewed, but it'll wash the supper down."

Sam's face beamed approval.

The Procter children and Kelly Walters had grouped themselves together beside a dry flint wall. Alison and Kelly had 'gelled' immediately. Kelly seemed to know about the wild flowers, and was busy pointing to types she claimed were rare. Tim just listened.

"They seem to be getting on," Sam said. "She gets on with most, but doesn't have too many friends. We live outside Lofton, see. She goes to the secondary school next term, things may change then."

Sam stood up and called over to the children. "Why not show Kelly the house?"

Bob Walters' eyes flicked upwards.

"Not for too long, though," Walters added. "We have to get back soon."

The three children tumbled across the bridge and disappeared into the house.

"So you've been having problems, I hear?" Bob Walters tried to look sympathetic.

Sam Procter held Walters' gaze, and sipped slowly at his mug of tea.

"Come on Bob, you're Geoff's brother, you must have heard the story. I arrive on site this afternoon after a long drive from London, to find one of the workmen half out of his tree because of some silly little accident."

"He was in that back bit, wasn't he?" said Walters. "Some room off the, the - what do you call it, Wheel House?"

"Yeah, so I understand," said Sam.

"He's a local - Jim Harris. Born and bred round here. This is a very old place, it has history and Jim has a sense of the past. Some of the others had been winding him up, see. He might have been a touch scared."

"Scared?" said Sam. "But of what?"

"Just stories."

"What kind of stories?"

"You know how folk talk. I'm telling you just so that you can take no notice of any silliness you may hear."

Sam wondered what he meant. He sipped more of his tea before continuing.

"And then Bill Smollett tells me that they are seriously behind with the second phase of the building work. Like two whole months behind!" Sam threw the rest of his tea against a rock.

"Geoff was talking about it earlier," said Walters. "It's not been their fault. They need some specialist scaffolding see, and they were let down. You've got to be careful with the foundations back there, requires experts. In all fairness to Bill Smollett, he didn't know that until they started to dig. That's the problems with digging stuff up, you don't know what you'll find."

He winked.

Sam put his mug down. He considered this for a moment, perhaps Geoff Walters had a point. Bob had obviously been sent here as a go-between - to help smooth things out.

"They're going to sort it for you, Mr Procter - Sam." Bob Walters lifted himself off his haunches and brushed down his apron. "Bill Smollett's a good builder, really."

Bob Walters did have the knack of smoothing things over. His voice, though deep and slightly gruff, made problems sound as if they could be solved.

"OK," said Sam Procter, looking across the bridge to see if the children had re-appeared.

"Just one thing. What did you mean about *stories*?"

"Come on, Mr Procter," laughed Bob Walters. "Every old place has stories, and we all know how much water they hold!"

Sam wasn't following this, then it occurred to him, could he be speaking about something else, something strange?

"Do you mean ghosts, and ghost stories?"

Walters laughed. "Lot of nonsense if you ask me!"

For some reason, Sam turned and looked back over the bridge. There was still no sign of the children. A slight wind caught the trees again and, for a few moments, the floodlights buzzed and dimmed. Behind the glass panels of the main doors, a spiral of silver mist twisted and vanished like smoke.

Sam Procter softly said the word again. "*Ghosts?*" He laughed. "I think it's time for bed."

Chapter 4

All Tim knew was that he was surrounded by darkness, and there was the constant breath of a soft distant whistle. At first he thought that the sound was that of a faraway train, because it had that lonely distant quality - of something travelling, and wanting to arrive. Whatever it was, it was on its way; it was coming.

Then the darkness fell away, like a curtain, and a wind rushed around him. The sky looked sick, a mottled and dirty yellow, with a huge shimmering sun that throbbed with the beat of his heart.

He felt as if he were floating over a strange landscape, pitted with streams of rushing dark water. At first the energy of the water was like that of the usual urgent gush, and then without warning, it would slow as if it were a tape recording that had suddenly jammed. The bubble and turmoil became something quite different - thick and slow like treacle. The noise of it drowned out the whistle, and it threatened to engulf him like a wave, to blot him out.

Tim sat upright with a start. Beyond the curtainless window, between the huge straight back of the Wheel House and the clump of trees, was the moon. It was full and pitted with specks of darker silver, with an aura that bled into the navy blackness of the starless sky. He looked across the room at his sister's cot bed;

she was fast asleep, her back to him.

As soon as his head hit the pillow, he was back. The faraway train was getting closer, the whistle now sounded even more like breath. But it was a single breath, long and certain, like a wheeze from a pair of old wet lungs.

Again, there was the bold image of the sun, but from behind this circle of light crept a blacker shadow, a sister disc that slid across the sky like a blade.

Now he could see the horizon - a level plain, with a boundary of trees, like figures on the perimeter of a field. He noticed that someone was watching him from the corner of his eye. He tried to see who, but the figure was always just out of sight, as if incapable of being seen directly. He noticed the corner of a raggedy coat, and a cowl. There was a face within. Perhaps the figure was now moving towards him?

Was that bleached white bone, darkly hidden within the cowl? Bleached white bone with clumps of grave earth in the eye sockets?

His eyes flicked open, and he caught his breath. He had been dreaming and his body was soaked in sweat.

Slowly, he turned towards the window. Something stood in the moonlight. It held a crooked staff in bony spider-thin fingers.

"No!" he screamed. And sat up yet again, dreaming within a dream.

The figure had gone.

His sister slept on.

Chapter 5

"Kelly was telling us about it last night," said Alison, her eyes wide and hungry for more gossip and tales, if there were any going. "This place is haunted. She said we were to keep it a secret and not to tell you, but she said everyone knows about it, so I thought it wouldn't matter."

Sam Procter poured a generous helping of cereal into their bowls. It was like eating in a 'TV advertisement' breakfast bar. Everything was shiny and new, with an unfinished row of kitchen cabinets. They helped themselves to provisions from a small cardboard box.

"So you know how to keep a secret, huh?" Sam said, peering through the window to check whether there was any sign of the builders. "It was a wonder you slept, hearing weird stories of boogie men late in the evening."

"Slept like a log," Alison quipped. She looked across at her brother, who had remained uncharacteristically quiet throughout breakfast. "And it wasn't a boogie man."

Tim looked over his bowl in silence.

"It's almost certainly a load of rubbish, old wives tales and the like. Actually Bob Walters did start to suggest that there might be a story or two about this place. He dismissed it all as nonsense as well."

Alison looked disappointed that her story might be ridiculed and spoiled.

Sam Procter heaved a huge sigh and went on. "I mean, there's no such things as ghosts. Everyone knows that."

Alison's face grew longer.

He could stand the suspense no longer. "Go on then, spill the beans, you're obviously dying to. What's he like, this ghost?"

"The ghost's a girl," Alison said. She was very matter-of-fact about it. "A serving maid."

Sam put down the milk and crossed over to where they were sitting. He considered her remark for a moment.

"I'm disappointed. Nothing nasty with chains that moans in the night, then? OK - carry on."

"Kelly's lived here all her life, the rumours and stories about the maid have been going around for years. When was the Victorian Age exactly, dad?"

Her father whistled through his teeth. "You mean you don't know? Well, let me see. That's the late part of the last century, let's say, give or take some years, from 1850 to the 1900's. That's a rough guide, could be a touch earlier or a bit later."

"Well Kelly said that the ghost is that of a Victorian serving maid, named Molly."

Sam pushed his chair back. She appeared to be taking all of this in her stride, but enthusiastically. Tim seemed quieter.

"Our ghost has a name then, Molly, anything else?"

Alison put her spoon down.

"Molly Gates. She worked here when Martyn's Mille was just a family house, in the Victorian times of course. Kelly said that the mill wheel hasn't been in use for hundreds of years, not since the 1700's."

"That's right," said Sam, as he fetched some sugar. "It's just been a grand family house with the land and the woods."

"Kelly says that local people talk of a strange accident. This serving girl went mad, said crazy things about the house and how the whole place was built on top of something terrible."

"Built on something?" He turned to look at her.

"Her master had her locked up," said Tim.

Tim's sudden remark struck a note into the conversation. All three looked at one another for a moment. Sam Procter pulled his chair closer.

"That's right," said Alison. "She was put in the County Asylum."

"But she escaped," said Tim.

"She came back to the house," continued Alison. "Nobody knew this until they found her some while after. Her body was discovered at the bottom of some steep stairs; those which lead down to the cellars of the Wheel House."

Sam nodded, he knew the steps. This had been where the builders had been having problems getting on with the work.

"The thing is. Well, she had died with this awful expression, so Kelly said," Alison swallowed uncomfortably, her enthusiasm for the story being replaced by a genuine dash of fear. "They couldn't get rid of this look on her face, her mouth all contorted and wide. That's what Kelly told us."

Alison's more casual tone had since departed, and despite the clear morning daylight, which generously filled the room, Sam Procter felt a chill about the place.

Tim wiped his mouth with a paper napkin. He kept looking about him as if expecting somebody. Sam started to gather the breakfast things together.

Alison continued. "Kelly said they tried everything to get the muscles in her face to relax. But they buried her in her coffin with this. . . well Kelly said locals called it a look of horror."

Sam put down the breakfast plates and picked up the mugs. Alison went on.

"Her aunt had wanted her to be in an open coffin in church, for the service before they buried her. But the Parson refused, and when the aunt arrived from Chesterfield, she understood."

"They said it would frighten the young children," Tim added.

Their father felt distinctly uncomfortable. The children had told the story too well. Far too well. Suddenly, he dropped one of the mugs. It rolled to the edge of the table, and crashed down on to the quarry-tiled floor.

"Damn," he cried. He watched as a puddle of milk slowly pooled across the tile, circling a small black spider that had been scuttling across the floor.

Alison ignored the accident.

"They say the girl's supposed to haunt Martyn's Mille, and sometimes people see her spirit in the ruins at the back, especially round the Wheel House."

"That's what Kelly told us," Tim added, his face showing no emotion.

Outside, Sam saw a builder's van arrive. He sighed with relief, and was very surprised to discover beads of perspiration on his forehead.

Chapter 6

"Right," said Sam Procter. "Come here, the pair of you, I want a word."

Tim and Alison joined their father on the forecourt. Behind him, Bill Smollett was directing two of his workmen. There was no sign of Jim Harris, the builder who had the accident. And no mention had been made of the driver who had nearly driven into them on their way to the mill.

"Just so's you know. Mr Smollett is re-scheduling the building works," said Sam. "He's expecting some new workmen too."

"Why?" asked Tim.

Alison jabbed him in the ribs, "Does it matter? You know dad's been having problems."

Bill Smollett joined them.

"My son wants to know why we are re-scheduling the work," said Sam, with a sparkle of mischief in his eye.

Bill Smollett cleared his throat and then his face broke into a wide smile.

"OK. Come on, I'll show you. Why not?"

He led the way to the far left-hand corner of the forecourt. The river almost became a stream at this point, and a makeshift bridge had been constructed out of planks.

"Across we go," said Smollett. "Be careful now. We'll be putting a proper bridge of some kind here later."

They continued across a small green, which was bounded by overgrown hedgerows. Up ahead was a cobblestone wall, part of which had obviously been re-built, the rest was in a state of reconstruction.

"This leads round to the courtyard at the back," said Sam. "The part you can see from the lounge."

They passed through an entrance which broke the line of the wall.

"I want to put a tall gate on here - wrought iron I thought."

"It's on order, Sam," said Smollett.

It was the first time that the children had stood in the courtyard. The wheel looked bigger somehow, and it was easy for Alison to see why her mother and father had fallen for the place. Below the wheel, the sound of the rush and tumble of the stream was clearer. Tim ran ahead and stood in the shadow of the huge spokes which stretched across the gravel. Alison watched him. He seemed to be standing in a shadow cage.

"OK," said Smollett, pulling Alison's arm as he pointed. "As you're interested. Part of the Wheel House, that tall bit of building to the left of the wheel, has to have some special underpinning."

"What's that?" asked Alison.

Tim returned, not wanting to be left out of interesting explanations.

"That means that the ground that all of that sits on has to be specially strengthened. Your dad wants us to build on to the Wheel House, see, to make the main restaurant room. Come with me."

Bill Smollett's control, and success in explaining the work to the children impressed Sam. He let him take the lead, trailing behind like a spectator on a tour.

Smollett took them down a bank beside the Wheel House. He pointed across the stream. The side of the embankment opposite had been cleared away, and a level beneath the floor of the upper building was revealed. Alison thought it was like the pictures in her encyclopaedia, where cut-aways showed how things worked. A row of steel bars supported lengths of timber.

"See those bars?" said Smollett. "That's all that's holding that lot up."

A look of concern flashed across Sam Procter's face. Smollett saw it. He crouched down and peered beneath the floor.

"Perfectly safe, Sam."

"It's like a tunnel under the house," said Tim.

Sam Procter stood and looked around him. The Courtyard did still look like a builder's yard, but he remembered it looking far worse when he was here a few weeks earlier. Perhaps Bill Smollett really was doing his best.

Tim had wandered further along the bank.

The fourth wall of the courtyard ended against the Wheel House, but there was another opening in the wall. Somebody had tried to block this up with an old door, which leant against the side pillars. Tim peered through the gap at the edges.

It was as if he had discovered a secret garden. An expanse of wild shrubland was pitted with what Tim took to be gullies or trenches, which seemed to fall at different levels.

Amongst all of this were ruins. But they were fabulous ruins, with large arches which ended in points, on which ivy and moss grew in wild weaving patterns. Crumbling walls were scattered at angles, with half-framed windows, as if they were the sole remains of an enormous abbey.

Sam and Bill Smollett noted Tim's interest, his face had been stuck in the gap for several minutes. Alison bounded forward and joined her brother.

"Hey, what have you found, let me see!"

The two men looked at one another.

"Looks like they've found the possible tourist attraction," said Sam Procter.

Bill Smollett suddenly stepped forward and grabbed Sam's arm. He turned and looked at him. Smollett's face was unsmiling and deadly serious.

"Remember what I told you, Sam."

"Lighten up Bill, they are only ruins."

"Just remember," said Smollett. "Just take care. Tell 'em they can play towards this end - but not in the Lower Quadrangle, that place near my big mixer."

For a moment Sam Procter could hear the sound of his own breathing.

"Take it easy Bill; and in any case they're my kids and they can play where they like. Darn it, I own all of this anyway."

Bill Smollett looked thoughtful, then spat at the ground.

"No Sam, you only own it with money, and there's some would say that isn't enough."

He sniffed and looked over his shoulder, back in the forecourt he could hear the voices of his workmen. He turned to go.

"By the way," said Sam. "Did you finish the tests on the Ducts - those in the Quadrangle?"

"They're all dry," said Smollett. "We had to take a great heavy iron door off one, then we chiselled a hole - no sign of any water still running. So if you get the 'OK' to fill it all in, I guess we can without too much complication."

"Thanks," said Sam.

Smollett rubbed his hands together and looked behind him.

"I've work to do," he said. "I'll do my best to catch up, Sam. A deal's a deal after all and I've my own reputation to keep."

Smollett left him. For a moment Sam considered what he had said to him, his comment suddenly rang in his head - 'some *would say that isn't enough.'* Was there some unspoken secret about this place? He decided that he probably meant nothing at all. For a second or two he smiled at Lancashire ways.

By now, Alison and Tim had removed the door beneath the archway.

Alison stared at the layout of the site. Trees marked out the boundaries - the whole area seemed to be a perfect square.

"This is the original mill," said Sam Procter proudly.

Alison looked surprised. "*Original mill*, but what's that next door then?"

"I told you this place was old, didn't I? The main building with the wheel is the mill that dated from the fire. At the start of the nineteenth century it was, or thereabouts. But this is where the original river was routed - see those tunnel things, aqueducts like drains?"

"Aqueducts? They're big enough to stand in," said Alison. "I've never seen anything like them before."

"Me neither. I'm told they were built by the original mill owners for maximum water power. It was thought that re-routing the river through these increased the force of the current. Sounded an interesting idea, don't know if it worked though. There are some lower levels too. We probably can't touch this part of the place, but I'm hoping to get a grant through the Tourist Board to develop it, perhaps an historical attraction."

"Can we play here? This is going to be great!" Alison danced and leaped over the trenches, peering down to see where the duct tunnels led.

"Be careful, perhaps it should really be roped off, but I don't suppose it's any worse than an adventure playground. I just can't understand how this site was overlooked by the local council."

"Perhaps it's been kept a secret," said Tim solemnly.

Sam looked thoughtful.

"Perhaps it has," he said, "*perhaps it has.*" Then he wondered why.

Up ahead was a central duct which was larger than any of its neighbours. With a skip, Alison jumped down onto a step and then into the hole.

"These make great play-pits!" she called.

Suddenly, she heard a voice behind her. It was almost a whisper. She turned and peered into the darkness. Someone was watching her.

Within the narrower part of the tunnel stood the dark figure of a girl.

Chapter 7

The girl turned, and within the shadows Alison recognised the peak of the baseball cap.

"Kelly!" cried Alison, and collapsed back against the duct wall. "You scared me half to death."

Sam Procter had rushed over and was gaping down at them.

"What's going on?"

A grimy, guilty-looking face, with deep brown eyes, peered out from the shelter of the tunnel. For a moment she wasn't sure whether she should smile or not. She had been holding something near her lips. Alison looked up at her father, then at her brother who now also stood beside him. She burst into laughter.

"Sorry," said Kelly, relieved that she might not be in trouble after all. "This is my hide-out, I play here sometimes when Uncle Geoff looks after me. Dad has to get his fish today from the market, his regular delivery was short. I'd left something here, I came back to get it."

She held up a stubby object, shaped like a tube.

"Up you come," said Sam, stretching out his arm to give her a hand.

"That's OK, I can manage," said Kelly, as she clambered out onto the other side.

"This is a really neat place," Alison gazed about her. A gentle breeze blew; it played with her hair, and as it crossed the open mouths of the ducts a barely discernible cry could be heard.

"Listen," said Tim, who was the first to hear it. They stood quietly.

The breathy, eerie voice of the breeze echoed through the aqueducts like a low moan.

"That's incredible," said Sam Procter. He had not heard this before.

"That's because they all join up," said Kelly. "It does that. If the wind is right you can stand in one place and call your name, and it can be heard right over the other side."

"I might employ you as a guide for this place, young lady," said Sam.

Tim and Alison peered through the main archway of cobblestone and brick. It bridged the ducts that ran across to the far side. Behind the clumps and mounds of hedgerow and wild shrub land, the limbs of the bordering trees shuddered.

Tim thought he heard something crack beneath his feet. He looked down, but it was nothing, just an old dry branch. The breeze blew stronger. He looked up again and felt his eyes drawn towards the far corner of the site. A light flashed, like a reflection in a mirror. Somebody dressed in a brown cloth, like an old gown or coat, stood amongst the trees. For a few moments the figure was as still as the tree trunks, then it moved and waved its arms at him. At first he thought that it might be beckoning, that the gesture was friendly, but for some reason he suddenly felt that it was not a friendly wave at all. Tim caught his breath and looked away. It reminded him of something.

"What's wrong?" asked Sam, noticing that his son had seemed to flinch.

He looked back for a second, partly afraid of what he might see, but there was only the sweeping arcs of branches.

"Nothing," he swallowed, then continued. "Is there a scarecrow or something like one over there?"

He looked up again.

"Your imagination," said Alison.

She sniffed the air and narrowed her eyes.

"This place is odd, isn't it?" she said. "I mean, it's different somehow."

Her father stroked the stubble on his chin. He had to agree, there was something about it, but it was impossible to pin-point. Why hadn't he noticed it before?

Kelly broke into a smile.

"I used to play here with my friend Jamie," she turned to Sam. "That was a long while ago, before you bought the mill, Mr Procter. Now I come here on my own, but it's more fun with friends, there's games you can play."

Sam wasn't sure about this. Previously he would have been happy to let his kids play in the ruins. But something had unsettled him. He wasn't sure what. Kelly smiled again and pulled her baseball cap more firmly on to her head.

"Then let's explore together," beamed Alison.

Tim had walked along the edge of the main duct and was staring ahead of him.

Sam Procter caught the faces of the two girls, standing together with an unspoken pleading expression.

"OK - but be careful and stay out of trouble. I've got to go into Lofton on business."

Sam looked at his watch, aware that he had spent longer here than he'd intended. He was about to make his way back to the house, when he suddenly heard a cry. Tim, who had been alone up ahead, threw his arms up in front of his face, and twisted round. For a few moments he didn't seem to recognise where he was. His eyes looked wild and he was in danger of falling into the nearby duct.

"Tim!" yelled his father.

Alison leapt across the duct and grabbed her brother. Kelly watched in silence.

"What is it, what happened?" Alison tried to hold him still. In an instant he seemed back from wherever he had been.

"I. . . I suddenly felt dizzy. It was the light I think."

"The light?" Sam Procter joined them. He held his son's head, checking to see if there were any untoward signs in his face.

"Somebody waved at me again," he said quietly, "from that corner, in the trees, then there were these spots of darkness behind the person."

Sam looked into his son's face again.

"Person? What person?"

Kelly smiled.

He looked across to the trees, but there was nobody there, only the breeze-blown shaking of branches entwined with moss.

"Come with me, we'll go into Lofton together, I want to keep one eye on you for now."

"I'm fine," said Tim. He tried to grin.

Kelly crossed to the spot where he had been standing. She stood with her feet slightly apart and surveyed the boundary like a general.

"There's nobody there, Mr Procter," she called back. "It might just be kids, but they don't usually come here. I think it was just the branches."

"Spots of darkness?" said Sam. "That sounds a bit to me like a headache starting up, something like a migraine. You'll be fine."

"Can we stay though?" asked Alison.

He hesitated.

"OK - but remember what Mr Smollett said, keep away from that area over there."

He pointed to where building supplies had been stacked.

"That's known as the Lower Quadrangle," said Kelly. "There's a small yard below the ground."

He raised his eyes to the skies. This girl

seemed to know the place like the back of her hand.

"Just keep clear. I'll tell your Uncle where you are, I won't be long."

They waved as Sam and Tim left to head towards the mill. Kelly stood watching them go, fingering the short length of tube she had been holding all this while. Slowly she lifted the tube to her lips, and blew. The wind moaned in response.

Chapter 8

Alison was alarmed by a cry from the sky. It was oddly like a child's wail. She looked up and shielded her eyes against the sun.

The noise came again, two short staccato stabs. It was the squawking of a bird. Above, a large black crow circled. At first it made small swoops and then the circles increased until it finally flew away, towards the farthest boundary of trees.

Kelly stood as still as the archway beyond, the wind twisting invisibly around her. For a split second it seemed as though the clouds were tumbling chaotically, one against the other. Kelly's eyes appeared to turn a deeper brown, and her gaze seemed deep and distant.

"Hey!" said Alison.

She rushed over and shook Kelly by the shoulder. Kelly lowered the tube from her lips.

"This was what you came here for, wasn't it?" said Alison, looking at the object. It might have been made of clay. It had several holes which were clogged with dirt.

Kelly nodded. Alison took the tube from her and tapped the side of it gently against a stone. More crumbs of dirt fell out.

"Did you hear the wind, just now? It rose when you blew this." Alison scratched away a section of dirt from the side.

"It didn't blow properly though," said Kelly.

"I mean it didn't make any sound like a proper whistle, though I've seen one like it before. I found this the other day."

"Where?" asked Alison. Kelly looked down at the ground, she was keeping something secret.

"It was around here, wasn't it?"

She nodded.

"But where?"

Kelly shook her head. "I might tell you later."

A thought crept into Alison's head. She half-suspected that Kelly had been exploring further afield, seeking out parts of the ruins she was supposed to keep away from.

"OK - but you know that I shan't tell, I mean if you want it to be *our* secret."

Kelly sniffed and smiled.

Alison continued to worry at the side of the whistle with her thumb-nail. At first she thought that she had discovered a pattern, or a drawing of some kind; but as she managed to scrape away more of the dirt, she saw that there were words.

"Do you know there's something written here? Come and see," said Alison.

She took out her handkerchief and spat in it. Then, she carefully cleaned the side. After a few moments the surface began to become cleaner and clearer.

"Ugh!" Alison exclaimed, almost dropping the thing.

"What's the matter?"

"I might be wrong, but take a close look at this," Alison held the object at arm's length; it had suddenly become something distasteful. "I think it's bone, and look at what's carved on the side."

Kelly watched closely as Alison scraped away more grime.

"Ye. . . Ye Summoner?"

She continued to look at the object with some disdain. Alison suddenly realised that Kelly didn't know what the word meant.

"Some of the letters are an odd shape, as if they're back to front. It's an old word, but I've heard it before, and recently too, in a story we read in school."

Kelly adjusted her baseball cap.

"Do you know the story of Aladdin and the Lamp?" asked Alison. "Well, he *summoned* the Genie by rubbing the lamp, so it's something you use to fetch or 'call up' something, like ringing a bell. So it must be a whistle then."

Kelly murmured in agreement.

Alison remembered that they had found Kelly with the whistle when they had arrived. And when the wind had changed and become strange, she had the whistle at her lips.

"Perhaps it does work," she said. "*Summoner.* I wonder what you've fetched?"

She looked beyond Kelly to the trees; the sounds of the builders behind her were peculiarly comforting. But the hammering and sawing seemed far off, almost as if in another world. The two girls stood closer together, and both found themselves turning towards the corner, searching out where Tim had seen his mysterious watcher.

Chapter 9

The journey to Lofton was longer than expected. Since leaving the mill, Sam Procter thought his son seemed nervous. They began by driving towards Lofton direct, passing through the tunnel of trees that made up Martyn's Place.

Tim kept switching his glances from the left to the right of the car, peering anxiously through the windows. It seemed that the fleeting glimpses of light through the leaves were bothering him. At the crossroads, midway through the woods, Sam made a decision and took the right turn, which although longer, took them out onto a higher road and through open fields. Tim preferred this, and settled.

Suddenly, Lofton rose abruptly from behind a low brow in the hill. It emerged like a rising sun, a brown and grey sprawl of rooftops which stood proud against the background of the V of the valley floor.

"There it is," said Sam. "Lofton. It's a friendly place, there are good people here, Tim," reassuring his obviously unnerved son.

Tim looked up at his father, and squeezed his arm.

They drove directly to the town square. It was busier today than Sam had remembered previously, and a row of market stalls reminded him of Kelly's remark about her father having to go to market for his fish.

He looked out for a parking place, driving slowly through seas of pedestrians, all of whom seemed to ignore the car.

"Why are we here?" asked Tim.

"Oh, I'm sorry," said Sam. "I hadn't told you. It's just to sign some forms at the Town Hall regarding the restaurant. I've also made friends with a chap in the planning department who is trying to sort out the legal status of the land at the back. He's OK, his name's Mr Brownsword."

"What do you mean, legal status?"

"You know - what we can do with it and what we can't. I hope that he's there today. They all seem to be in a bit of a muddle about it. Martyn's Mille has just gone to ruin over the years, official paperwork included. Sometimes there's this older woman who tries to be as unhelpful as possible. Between you and me, I don't think she approves of the restaurant plan."

Sam spotted a space at the far side of the square, where a Land Rover was pulling out.

"There's a spot," he said. "Here we go."

They parked, and walked back through the square. Overlooking the market stalls was a squat building with steps. It seemed to Tim that Town Halls looked the same everywhere.

"Do you want to wait here, or come in with me? There's a bench over there if you'd like."

"I'd like to come in with you," he replied immediately, almost too quickly.

Sam paused.

"Are you alright, Tim?" he asked. "I mean, you had a bit of a scare didn't you?"

"I'm OK, it's just. . ." he struggled to explain, but suddenly wasn't sure what there was to explain. Nothing had really happened. He sighed instead, "Never mind."

Sam stared at his son for a moment. Together, they climbed the steps to the Town Hall.

Lofton Town Hall was a building of dark panelled walls, flaky cream-painted ceilings and the eternal echo of footsteps, tapped out on diamond shaped tiles. There was a mysterious hush about the place, as if occupants were under some kind of special instruction to speak only in raised whispers. Tim felt uncomfortable, and for a moment wished he had remained outside.

"This way," said Sam. "Along this corridor."

They turned into a passage which stretched as far as Tim could see. Brown doors with frosted glass panels lined the passage at equal intervals, and occasionally there were polished wooden benches beside the doors.

"Here we are, the Planning Office." Sam Procter almost gritted his teeth as he said it.

He pressed a white button on a bell push and sat down on the bench.

"It's a big place," said Tim, peering down the

corridor as he sat beside him. Further along, an old woman dressed entirely in black was hunched on a bench, her face hidden by a shawl. Tim looked back at the woman a second time.

After a moment the door opened and a short red-faced man with a grey waistcoat and a big smile of teeth, appeared.

"Mr Procter, isn't it? How nice to see you again, please do pop in. And who is this?"

The man offered his hand to Tim, and pushed his face towards him. He smelt of aftershave, and thinning hair had been parted to hide the bald crown.

"I'm Tim," he said. "Tim Procter."

"And I'm Mr Brownsword."

Mr Brownsword held the door open for them.

They entered a small room where there was another door of frosted glass behind a desk. Tim could see the shapes of people behind the glass, busily rushing about. He heard the click-clack of keyboards being punched, and an occasional giggle and laugh which revealed a secret world of people.

Mr Brownsword gestured for them to take a seat at the desk, and then he joined them. He produced a large blue folder from nowhere and after popping a pair of half-moon glasses on the end of his nose, he examined several forms.

"Here you are, Mr Procter," he said. "I think you'll find this all in order. This document is to request the licence, and the other is related to the Committee's approval for your extension. I gather you've started already, but we agreed that over the phone, didn't we? Just between us."

He smiled a full smile.

Sam Procter took the forms and looked them over for a moment. Then he took a pen offered by Mr Brownsword and signed the bottom of each sheet.

"Splendid," said Mr Brownsword. "I must say it'll be a pleasure to see your restaurant, your alterations sound most interesting. It'll be nice to have a special place to visit too, for that 'night out'. Mrs Brownsword and myself have to go all the way to Siddersmouth, to the Royal Huntsman Hotel if we want anything special to eat, you know, for an anniversary or something." He leaned forward. The aftershave smelt stronger.

Sam Procter smiled and put the cap on the pen.

"Er, Mr Brownsword," Sam looked up and held Mr Brownsword's gaze for a moment. "Have you any news for me on that other matter, the rear site of Martyn's Mille?"

Mr Brownsword sucked through his teeth, and tapped the forms neatly into a pair on the table edge.

"That's a minor embarrassment still, Mr Procter, a minor embarrassment."

Tim looked up with interest, the paper processing so far had been boring.

"It does seem as though some important papers relating to the site have, well, shall we say, gone walkies somewhere."

"Gone walkies?" repeated Tim.

"Shush," said Sam. "Excuse my son."

"No - they're missing still," said Mr Brownsword. "As far as I can tell there were these folks, about a couple of years or so ago, who were considering turning the place into some kind of nursing home, a local couple by all accounts - a Mr and Mrs Dunn. But they didn't proceed. That was the last time the archives had been retrieved."

"I didn't know that," said Sam. "I thought I had been the first person to show any interest in developing the mill for years."

"So you are," said Mr Brownsword. "And so you are. Except for the Dunns."

"Why didn't they carry out their plans?" asked Sam.

Mr Brownsword shook his head. "No record of the reason. But they did ask for some fairly old parish documents. It was a job turning them up. To be honest Mr Procter, those things were so old that they had to be traced through the Lofton Museum and Historical Society. I was in another department then."

Sam Procter nervously tapped the table top with his fingers.

"So you've no news on what I can renovate, and what I can't? I've got this plan, see."

"Not at the back bit Mr Procter, not yet," he

said. "Sorry, but I hope to have some news for you fairly shortly. It's embarrassing really, we're usually such an efficient little section."

Sam lowered his voice.

"I'm having a spot of trouble getting the Wheel House work completed. I thought I might be able to get the builders advanced on some other project in the meanwhile, a sun trap idea for the rear."

"We know builders, Mr Procter," said Mr Brownsword. "But you've got a good firm with Smollett, pity a few of the men got the heebie-jeebies about the mill."

Sam looked up suddenly. Tim pushed his arm against his father's.

"Heebie-jeebies?" Sam repeated.

Mr Brownsword burst out laughing.

"Just my little term, means nothing. Place has a little history - you know that, I'm sure."

"You mean the ghost?" said Sam.

Mr Brownsword pushed his chair back and stood up.

"Ridiculous stories, Mr Procter. Ridiculous. Welcome to Lofton - it'll be grand to see a spanking new restaurant here."

Mr Brownsword was quick to push his hand out for Sam to take. He smiled down at Tim.

"Be a good lad, now. Look after your dad. I'll be in touch, Mr Procter."

He went round the table and opened the door for them to leave. A whoosh of stale air hit the smell of aftershave, which lingered in the room. Within moments they were alone in the corridor, no tapping of footsteps echoed elsewhere. The place seemed suddenly deserted.

"That's it then," said Sam looking down at his son.

Tim glanced to his left; the old woman in black was no longer there. Instead, somebody else - also awkwardly hunched, now sat on the bench, in a long brown dress. His breath caught at the back of his throat as he stared.

"Come on, we'll see the market," said Sam, as he led Tim along the corridor to the exit. He went with his father, resisting the urge to look back at the bench. His father hadn't appeared to have noticed the old woman.

As they turned the corner, Tim *did* look back. But she had gone.

Chapter 10

"So, how do you play this then?" asked Alison.

She kept looking upwards. Perhaps it was because the walls were so steep. They were, after all, standing in what Kelly claimed was one of the deepest parts of the aqueduct, at the centre of the site.

"OK - now listen carefully," began Kelly. She sat on a ledge, formed out of a jag of flint rock in the wall. "We used to call this '*if you don't come to me, I will come to you.*' It's a great game."

"Who was the '*we*'?" asked Alison.

"I told you," grinned Kelly, "that was me and Jamie, we played here sometimes."

"And what about the title, who thought that up?"

Kelly gave a false yawn, "Are we going to get on and play this or not? The title is real old, Jamie's mum told us. I mean I didn't make it up. We take turns. I'll go first if you like, since I know the passages."

Alison crossed her arms and waited for further explanation.

"Right, it's like this. You turn and face the wall, we always start from this point at the beginning. I go off and find a place somewhere in the ducts, it could be right over the other side. After five minutes or whatever time we agree, you come and find me. The thing is though, whilst you're trying to hunt me out I'm also trying to find you - it's a matter of who gets to who first."

Alison thought about this for a moment. It sounded very unusual, chasing after one another, uncertain who was the hunter and who was the hunted.

"A few other things," Kelly continued. "I will stop every now and then and call out something to you, it could be just a yell or your name. If a breeze blows up top it carries the message through the passages, but it can get confusing. That's the fun of it, you see. You might think someone is just round the next bend, when in fact they are in another passage behind you!"

Alison nodded. "How do we know who has won, I mean how do we know who has caught who?"

"Whoever sees the other person first has to be quick off the mark. They point and say '*Old Mother Gudgeon has got you*'. If I say it to you first, then I'm the winner."

Kelly's face was wide-eyed. Her explanation of the game had been very matter-of-fact, it was obvious that she had played this many times before.

"Why do we say that?" Alison asked, "I mean why not just something plain and ordinary, like - 'gotcha'?"

"It's the tradition, I told you it was an old game," said Kelly, feeling mildly irritated by so many questions. "I don't really know why we say that, but we just do, it's how it was played in the old days. Come on. Give me five minutes then?"

"Alright." Alison didn't feel as enthusiastic as she felt she should.

She looked at her watch.

"It's easy-peasy," sang Kelly. She disappeared down a length of tunnel, and round a corner.

For a moment Alison puzzled over who 'Old Mother Gudgeon' might be. Something inside her suggested that she might not want to know, the name somehow sounded nasty.

She looked upwards again, just noticing the tip of the arch which rose above the duct. It looked like a giant finger, pointing towards the sky. Feeling suddenly dizzy she looked down and faced the wall.

A worm slowly wriggled out from between the rocks near her face, and she stepped back with a small cry. Surely she didn't have to remain standing there, simply looking at earth? She decided to turn around.

Alison felt very alone.

The world above had become silent and distant, as if it were another place in another time. All of a sudden overhead, a warm gust blew by. It carried her name, "*Alison,*" and vanished into the sky.

There was a split second of silence.

Alison swallowed, her mouth had dried. She reached out to the side wall to steady herself.

The cry came a second time; it didn't sound

like Kelly's voice at all, but she knew it had to be her.

For a moment the call of her name had hovered above, seemingly in the air. Then it was as though the walls had become invisible - and she could actually see Kelly's outline through the walls, two ducts away.

"Is that you, Kelly?" she spoke in a hushed, nervous voice; then shook her head and the image faded.

She had not bothered to look at her watch, or counted minutes or seconds. Time had passed slowly.

"That must be five minutes by now," she thought. "I'd better start. But where?"

Alison considered the passage ahead; several ducts offered options. For a moment the choice confused her, but with a determined rush, she took off.

Without thinking, she let her feet take her forward and made a left turn and ran. There were less covered sections here, and the stretch was longer. She ran on for some way.

After a while she slowed her pace and walked. Somewhere above her came the whirl of another passage of air - almost breath.

"*Alison,*" said the voice, more softly this time.

She stopped short - it was as if her name had been called from inside her head. She turned on her heels. Just behind her, to the right, she glimpsed a hand on the corner of a rock.

Fingers were spread wide, for seconds only.

"Kelly!" she cried with a smile, and dashed back down the duct after her, like a hare.

She turned into the passage. It was rough, clumps of stone getting in her way, and there was no sign of Kelly. Up ahead was a stretch of cover. The duct also narrowed here, but she was unable to see the sides of the walls. It seemed to be rapidly getting darker.

She stopped.

"Kelly?" she whispered.

She moved forwards cautiously, just in case she might be surprised.

"What am I supposed to say?" she whispered to herself, trying to remember: *'Old Mother Gudgeon has got you'.*

She stopped again and listened. She could hear only her heart beating, the pitter-patter that drowned out the silence of everything else.

Further on. She must go further on.

Was that a sound behind her, a rustle like the brush of rough linen? She spun round. There was nobody. One step at a time, she edged further forward, into the darker part of the duct.

All of a sudden, her feet felt wet, and each step seemed to press into something soft and yielding like mud. Again she rested, and listened, but there was still only the sound of her heartbeat. She looked straight ahead, for some reason she dared not look to the sides.

She took another step.

It was going to be alright, there was nothing to be afraid of, surely?

But from the left somebody called her name.

She turned her eyes towards the sound. There in the darkness, she saw two pin-point pricks of red. They glowed, like animal eyes, yet somehow colder and more dangerous. She was still unable to see the sides of the wall - they might have stretched back forever. She caught her breath, and for some reason reached out her hand.

Then the hand of another gently held her own; she felt thin fingers, cold and brittle and damp.

Alison shrieked.

The smell of wet earth filled her nostrils, and she felt as though something thick and cloying had rushed into her mouth.

The soft, squelching sensation around her feet increased, as though something thick and maybe sticky had seeped through the floor of the passage.

"Kelly!" she cried, "where are you? Help me, *Please!*"

She turned and with a simpering cry rushed back down the duct. This time it was blind panic, running anywhere to get away, but from whom or from what?

"Alison," her name was called again.

"No - oh no," she resisted the urge to sob, to break down. She took a deep breath and clenched her fist. She looked up. For a moment she glimpsed the sun, then the edges dripped into the clouds, as though it was a disc of melting wax.

Something scuffled around the corner to the left. Without thinking, running blind, she took off again, straight round the turning.

She ran into gloom once more.

And then she stopped dead, her heels digging hard into the earth.

She saw a shape, a silhouette that stood silently in the centre of the duct ahead. Alison was frozen with fear. But, it must be Kelly - there was nobody else down here.

"Old Mother Gudgeon has got you." She found herself croaking out the message - the cry of the victor, but her mouth tasted salt dry.

The shape did not move, not a word was spoken.

"Kelly," she whispered. "That is you - isn't it? Please say it is, don't do this. *'Old Mother Gudgeon has got you.'"*

From behind her she heard the message repeated, but it was a different, kinder voice. She twisted on her heels and saw Kelly, her brown eyes dark and piercing - but for a second nothing made sense, Kelly was *behind her*.

Slowly, her heart in her mouth, she turned back to face the owner of the other voice, which was ahead of her.

"Now it's dark," said the voice.

Chapter 11

Tim was relieved to be back outside, breathing fresh Lofton air again. The stuffiness and heat of the Town Hall had filled his head with a fuzzy feeling, as if it were full of clumps of cotton wool. His father had glanced down at him once or twice, puzzled at his son's mood. Tim kept quiet, still struggling with the uncertainty of whether he was imagining things or not.

Whilst his father went to buy a newspaper, Tim stood in the square and watched the people pass by. Was it possible that he was seeing things, or that ordinary people and events just simply appeared different and strange?

For a moment he remembered back to when he was smaller. An old lady had stood at the corner of their road almost every day for a week, selling bunches of heather to passers-by. He remembered how she had bothered him; how just her presence had worried at him like a nagging itch. It was something about her face, the way she looked and the strangeness of her big billowing purple skirt. Once she had worn a head scarf, and from certain angles she appeared as though she was deliberately hiding her face.

He had told his parents that she was watching him. His mother had told him not to be so ridiculous. One afternoon he had looked out of his bedroom window and had caught her looking up at him - he was sure of it. He had pulled the net curtain closed suddenly, and when he had peeked out a few moments later, she had gone. He never saw the woman again, and Alison had told him not to be so silly, and to be more grown up about things.

'Be more grown up about things.' Her remark rang in his head once more.

"Shall we see the market Tim?" asked Sam Procter, re-appearing out of a small crowd of shoppers.

Tim tried to smile.

Since they had been inside the Town Hall, the square had become busier. The odd passer-by nodded at Sam, and he had raised an eyebrow in return, or waved at people Tim had never seen before. His father had obviously started to make connections.

There were all kinds of stalls, piled high with fresh vegetables and fruit. Trestle tables stood everywhere, crowded with what Tim thought might be junk, but which his father had called bric a bric - and 'perhaps antiques'.

Towards the water fountain were a row of temporary wooden shelves, beside cardboard boxes, overflowing with stacks of second-hand books and magazines. They stopped to look for a moment. A box on one table was filled with very old books, in rusty brown covers. Sam paused at this table, and flipped through the pages of one particular dog-eared volume. It was larger than the others, and was filled with black line drawings of country scenes and maps. Tim peeped over his father's arm and strained to see the title, *"Lofton - its Customs and Lore."*

Suddenly, Tim saw somebody he recognised through the crowd. He tugged at his father's sleeve and pointed. Through the milling group of shoppers, with two hefty carrier bags in each hand, was the unmistakable form of Kelly's father, Bob Walters - the fish and chip man.

"Go on," said Sam. "Whilst I get this, go and tell him we're here."

He skipped off through the crowd towards Walters. At first he didn't recognise Tim, who bounced up to him as if he were a long lost friend.

"Well I never," said Walters, shifting one of his carriers over to his other hand. He reached out to slap Tim on the shoulder.

"Young Mr Procter, of course, we had fish and chips last night."

Tim beamed a smile up at him. There was something deeply comforting about Bob Walters, almost as if he were everybody's favourite uncle.

"Dad's through here," said Tim. "He's buying a book. Kelly's back at our place."

"I should hope so," said Walters. "Hope your dad don't mind, my brother keeps an eye on her sometimes."

Through the crowd came Sam Procter, a brown paper parcel under his arm, along with the envelope of documents given to him by Mr Brownsword.

The two men nodded. Then Walters lifted his carrier as if to show Sam.

"Fish," he said.

"Er, book," said Sam Procter, feeling as if he should oblige with some revelation himself. They laughed. "Got it on that stall back there. It's a book about Lofton, pretty old by the look of it."

Walters raised an eyebrow and looked past him. "I knew the feller that used to run that business, does summat else now. He seemed to have the knack of finding some real strange books. There were a lot goin' round years ago about this area, and he kind of specialised in local stuff. Has a history - this place, as you probably know. Lancashire and Pendle and the old witch trials of the Middle Ages. Lofton's been involved with some odd tales. At one time he had his stall stacked up with these funny old metal bound things that told you how to cure warts on your nose, or charm a local lass to fall in love with you! Not so much now, I think you'll find them big fat modern novels and other things there. Nowt too weird and wonderful."

Tim seemed pleased to see Walters. For a moment Walters seemed to be considering whether to continue, his tongue licked his lower lip, then he coughed.

"You know," he went on. "Funny thing really, I mean you going and buying a book from there. I can't resist making a connection."

"Why's that?" asked Sam.

Walters gestured with his head that they should move to the side. It was becoming increasingly crowded, and they had stopped to talk in a thoroughfare.

They ambled over to a clearer spot. A nearby pub had already opened, and sets of tables had been put out on the front. Coffee and tea was being served to shoppers and a few of the market traders had begun the day with a frothy pint.

"Have a seat," said Walters. "I gotta go shortly, but I picked up my extra fish a bit sharper than usual today - I can spare a bit of time."

Tim saw that his father was intrigued. If Walters was anything like his daughter, tales were going to tumble.

He sat quietly for a moment, as though he needed prodding. Sam obliged.

"You were saying, something about the book stall? The owner?"

"I just had a moment of second thoughts about saying 'owt," he said. "That's all. But what the heck. Well as I said, the lad what owned that pitch was a mate of mine. His boy used to hang around with my Kelly, nice kid - Jamie was his name. But the little coincidence is that he was the only man round these parts who had considered buying Martyn's Mille."

A wry smile crept across Sam Procter's face. He leant forward and looked Bob Walters full in the face. Tim watched quietly.

"Couple of years or so ago, wasn't it? His name wasn't Dunn by any chance?"

Walters sat back in his seat and laughed quietly. His laughter had a nervous edge to it.

"Nowt seems to get past you Mr Procter - I'll give you that. Yes - John Dunn, wife's name Mary. They had this over-ambitious plan to convert the mill into some sort of nursing home, or something of the like. She's a qualified nurse, see. It was to be her little business venture."

"We've just been to the Town Hall," said Tim. "A man in the office told dad."

"Ah," said Bob Walters.

"Why didn't they buy dad's mill?" asked Tim.

Walters sniffed and looked about him, he seemed slightly bothered by the question. "So your Town Hall lad didn't tell you?"

Sam leant forward, placing his hand gently on his son's arm. Tim realised he was to keep quiet.

"No," said Sam. "They just said that no reason was given."

"I think it was simply unsuitable in the end. Nowt else to it."

"Our man at the Town Hall also seemed to

have heard about our problems with the builders. What was it he said now? Something about some of the men getting the, er, the 'heebie-jeebies' was the expression."

Bob Walters began to gather up his carriers.

"I'd better get these fish out of the sun and into my van."

Sam Procter reached out and placed his hand on Walters' arm.

"What did he mean, Bob?" Sam persisted with his questioning.

"Oh probably nothing, just local stuff."

"The ghost perhaps? Come off it, ever since I got back here I've felt as if I've been given some kind of run-around, and it doesn't all add up. You suggested something about it last night when you called, it's as though you want to explain and then you bottle out. Anyhow, your daughter told my kids the story. All about it."

He froze. "All about it? Never you mind young Kelly - she's got a mouth the size of the Lofton Valley." He slapped his hand on the table. "What did she say, was it about the girl, the serving girl?"

"Yes," said Sam. "What's her name - Molly something?"

"Yes, yes you're right."

Tim watched carefully. Bob Walters appeared relieved to hear his father's admission. "Tell me about it, Bob. Come on. I wasn't born yesterday. You called round last night to smooth things over - I know that, and it was OK that you came. But your brother's the foreman for Smollett, and I know that Bill Smollett wants this contract as much as I want him to finish it! The men need the work. I know how things have been round here."

Walters nodded slowly. "Times have been tough, I admit it, we need the work and my brother needs to remain Bill Smollett's foreman."

Sam leaned back in his chair and grinned. "I wouldn't be surprised if even nice Mr Brownsword in the Planning Department is smoothing things over to get some new life into Lofton. Work all round eh, and perhaps there are even backhanders involved. Let me tell you, getting this off the ground has been fairly easy, so let's scratch each others' backs. And let's have some facts. This ghost story - is there any truth in it?"

Bob Walters laughed. "I'll be straight with you Mr Procter. Who knows whether there are any such things as ghosts? You're an intelligent man, you know as well as I do that nowt's proven."

Sam drummed his fingers on the table. Tim listened in fascination.

Walters went on. "Yes, there's a story. Kelly told you that, she probably livened it up a bit too, if I know her. She had no business saying owt. What do you know?"

Walters held Sam's gaze with a steel-eyed stare.

"That the place is supposed to be haunted by this serving girl, who died by falling down some stairs."

"Well, that is it in a nutshell. There's the odd fancy turn on the story as to how she died with this horrible look on her face."

"And has anyone seen this ghost?" asked Sam.

Tim moved closer. The hum of life in the market place had seemed to decay. It was as though there were only the three of them.

Walters lowered his voice. "There's those that claim to have. Sometimes she's seen in the ruins, and sometimes in that back bit - the Wheel House. She's not seen that much though, until you bought the place nobody went anywhere near it. Except my daughter that is, she played there for a bit with the Dunn's boy when they were thinking of buying it."

"So - the Wheel House. Where the builder had the accident with the drill?"

Walters nodded. Tim thought he was becoming restless.

"Come on," said Sam. "That's where he thought he saw something, didn't he? The lights went out or what have you?"

Bill Walters moved closer. "Look Mr Procter, I'm looking after my brother's interests - if Bill Smollett knew I was saying owt he'd have my guts."

"It's OK," said Sam. "Let me guess then - so

you don't need to admit anything. I think it goes something like this: The odd workman or two has been getting carried away with hearing stories about this ghost. One or two think they see her, have an accident and so on. I arrive at an unfortunate and inconvenient time. Mr Smollett quite rightly thinks it's best to keep all of this from me in case I think he's got a loony work force. Perhaps he has. The reason for the slow down of work on the rear of the mill has been because of these stories. Now, your brother and Mr Smollett try and keep the workmen sweet by rubbishing the tales, but even so they are having to bring in a gang from elsewhere to work at the back, because some of his own men are too scared to work there. Let me see now, the new lot will probably be contracted from elsewhere - workmen who couldn't care less about ghost stories. In other words not locals, and that's where we are to date. Am I right?"

Walters nodded. "You've got it, Mr Procter. But all will be OK now, the men will be arriving any day."

"And what's all this about special scaffolding or something?"

"That's true. It's to give them more room to work beneath the Wheel House. Bill Smollett thinks it's the small space that gets to them. Anyway - they'll get on faster with the new stuff."

"So it's all down to the ghost of some serving

maid?"

"I guess so."

"What a load of nonsense."

Walters appeared to liven up. "That's right - but there's nowt so queer as folk - as the saying goes."

Sam shook his head from side to side.

"Don't say anything to Smollett," said Walters. "Please, my brother needs that job."

Sam smiled. "Just so long as I know."

Tim began to crack his knuckles. One by one. Walters glanced at him with an uncomfortable look. Then he checked his watch and gathered his carriers together.

"I must go. So - it's all settled then?"

Sam looked up at him. He caught the look on his son's face. Tim stopped playing with his knuckles. He looked worried and confused.

"Yes, yes - that's it Bob. I'll be seeing you."

Bob Walters scurried away into the crowd. He had behaved as though he had scored some kind of victory.

"Anything the matter, Tim?" said Sam, as he stretched his legs to get up.

"That Mr Walters wanted you to believe that the ghost was Molly Gates, didn't he? I mean he wanted you to believe that really badly, even though he was joking about it all being silly stories."

Sam stared back at his son. Walters' attitude had changed strangely. Could Tim be right?

Tim bit his bottom lip and frowned. "But the question is, why?"

Chapter 12

Alison saw the shape for just a second. At first she thought it was a shadow. But there was the voice - low and insistent, but with a frightening urgency about it.

Then she saw the face, contorted into a mask of pure dread.

It spoke again: *"Now it's dark."*

Then, it floated out of the shadows. As she had thought, it was a girl, but older than herself by several years. She appeared translucent, and somehow delicate. It was as though she had been peeled from out of an old brown-faded photograph. She wore a serving girl's uniform of an older era, a white pinafore and lace ruffled hat with a black dress.

She reached out her arms towards Alison, who felt unable to move, not even to look over her shoulder to check that Kelly was behind her.

Suddenly, the figure behaved as though she was elsewhere, not in the trench at all. She raised her hands to the sides of her face and looked down. She gave Alison the impression that she might be looking over the edge of something, maybe down a staircase.

She turned her face towards Alison and gave a long and horrible screech. It echoed into the distance, as if it were travelling into an abyss. The girl appeared to fall forward, as though she had stumbled - but she fell *through* Alison.

Alison cried out, and clawed at herself, thinking for a split second that the girl had somehow entered her own form. Beneath the sandy surface of the ground she saw the girl sailing down and down - into the darkness of the earth.

She looked up, and without a second thought ran ahead as fast as she could. A voice called to her from behind.

"Alison - wait! It's me, Kelly!"

But she ignored the cry and rushed forward, aware only of a heartbeat that blotted out the sound of everything else.

"Alison - please, the game's over!" Kelly's calls were in vain. Alison heard nothing. Kelly made certain that her whistle was secure in her pocket, and decided to take off after her.

Alison saw only the sides of the duct as they rushed past her. Shadowy gloom loomed up ahead.

The thumpety-thump in her ears grew louder, she felt her heart would burst. Tears started to bubble up in her eyes, making it even more difficult to tell where she was going. It was like seeing through a rippling opaque sheet of glass, forever changing.

Suddenly, she ran into a wall of red clay. Overgrown moss and weeds hung down from above, forming a web-like skein of hair. She swallowed hot air with large gulps, then turned and headed down to the right.

There was light at the end of this tunnel. The promise of sunshine danced across the end wall, the shadows of branches flickered across the surfaces. She could just make out bricks, or cobblestones - there was something more solid here, not mere damp earth.

Finally, she reached the end and fell against the stone. Her hands pressed against the coolness, she felt her cheek push into the comfort of something strangely assuring. She had closed her eyes, and when she opened them she realised that the duct had opened out into a large enclosed space - like a small yard. As though in a drunken faint she staggered forward into the space.

The first thing she did was to look upwards. The walls here were steep, much higher than the walls of the ducts. The sky was blue and clear, it looked less angry here than it did in other parts of the aqueduct system. For a moment she felt she might be safe.

She swallowed back the rest of her tears and sat down on a stone seat that jutted out from the wall. Then she noticed the floor. It wasn't made up of dirt brown soil that was the character of the ducts elsewhere. This floor was tiled, with a mosaic of tiny diamonds and squares. For some reason the pattern engrossed her immediately. She turned her head to the side. The effect was patchworked, as clusters of ingrained dirt and weeds, which sprouted from cracks, confused the effect of the whole. She thought that it might make up a circle with stars in it.

All of a sudden she heard a voice. Startled, she looked up and stared about her. It was only then that she realised that a whole cluster of ducts ended here. She felt as if she were at the centre of a maze.

The voice came again - this time it sounded from the right. She caught her breath as an outline appeared, a girl stood in the passageway of the duct opposite. She could breath again. Although the baseball cap was now pushed further back on her head, it was clear who it was.

"Alison," cried Kelly. "Why didn't you stop? I told you the game was over, I've been following you for ages!"

Alison stood up, ran over to Kelly and gave her a big hug. Kelly seemed surprised.

"Hey, what was that for?"

"Just to make sure that you're real," said Alison. She pushed the hair away from her eyes.

"Of course I'm real," said Kelly. "Why did you run off like that? I'd found you after all."

Alison stood back for a moment and looked Kelly up and down. She didn't appear to be upset at all.

"You didn't see it, did you?" she said.

"Didn't see what?" said Kelly, readjusting her own hair.

"The girl, the figure - in the passage. She

screamed too, don't tell me you never heard that?"

"I heard *you* scream," said Kelly. "It almost frightened the daylights out of me, and there I was. . ."

She trailed off, Alison was stern-faced.

"You really did see something, didn't you?"

Alison nodded furiously and fought back a further outburst of tears. "Back there, it was the ghost, I'm certain of it."

"What did she look like?" asked Kelly. "I mean what was she wearing, was it a white dress, with flowers - was she holding flowers, and was she tall?"

"No," said Alison softly. "No - that wasn't her, not at all. She had a black maid's dress on, with a white hat and pinny. She was a bit taller than me - but not much."

"You saw her alright," said Kelly. "I was just testing you."

"This isn't a joke," said Alison angrily.

"I know," said Kelly. "But I'm not to know, am I? Not everyone sees her, you've got to be a certain kind of person. And. . ."

"And what?" Alison snapped.

"Hey, take it easy," said Kelly. "I'm sorry, I didn't mean to doubt your word. But there was a time when all kinds of kids round here were claiming to see Molly. I was only going to say that there's some that say she sometimes only appears to certain people. Did she say anything to you?"

"She did," said Alison. For a moment the memory of the encounter made her shudder. She stepped back and sat on the seat again. "She said 'Now it's dark'. It was a strange thing to say - but it made me shiver."

"Do you know what it means?"

"Of course not!" Alison replied sharply. "Tell me something. Two things, firstly - have you ever seen her?"

"No," said Kelly, almost with a note of disappointment in her voice. "I don't think I'm the right sort. But Jamie, my friend, he said that he saw her a couple of times. She seemed to be staring into the ground, as though she was about to topple over."

"That's it," said Alison. "If she was found at the bottom of the stairs then she was probably reliving her death. Poor thing."

Kelly paced the floor. "You said there were two things, what was the other?"

"With this game, you mentioned that you call out every so often. What did you call out to me?"

"That's easy - 'I'm on my way,' that's what I called, in a funny voice - you know, just for fun!"

Alison leaned back against the wall. "You never called my name?"

"No," said Kelly. "Just, 'I'm on my way', or 'I'm coming', I changed it once or twice - just a bit."

Alison looked thoughtful for a moment and then sighed.

"Are you scared?" Kelly asked.

Alison thought about this for a second. "No. No I don't think so. I *was* scared though, back there in the ducts - I mean it can get really spooky down there. I prefer it here, it's like a courtyard garden."

"That was the fun of playing here, the spookiness," said Kelly.

"So what happened with Jamie?"

"Oh - his mum and dad stopped him from playing with me, they said I got strange sometimes. Huh. They used to spend a lot of time looking about the mill. Jamie said that they were thinking of buying the place, they were going to change it into something, not a restaurant though - that's the neatest idea yet. Jamie started having these dreams and things, and his mum called me a 'bad influence'."

She laughed.

"I don't think you're a bad influence," said Alison.

Kelly gave an impish grin and sniffed. Alison paced the floor of the yard, it suddenly occurred to her that they had emerged here - into a strange area that appeared to have no purpose.

"Where are we - what is this place?" Alison looked at the floor again. This time the pattern seemed clearer - there were crescent shapes, and stars scattered within the design of the tiles.

"This is known as the Lower Quadrangle," said Kelly. "We shouldn't be here really, this is the place that Mr Smollett warned us off."

Alison peered down one of the aqueducts. The air seemed to shimmer above the ground. She thought it was an effect of the heat, like a desert mirage.

Then she noticed that between the ducts was a lower opening, about waist high. She bent down and peered into one of them. A grid had been fixed over the front. She crouched down and looked inside, it was pitch black and somewhere in the distance she could hear a gentle rush like water.

She stood up. "I wonder why we were told not to come here?"

"I guess because it's the main reservoir," said Kelly, in a matter-of-fact voice.

"How do you mean?"

"Well, Jamie once said that they thought this was the kind of engine for the aqueduct system. The place where all the energy for the mill was stirred up."

Alison turned, she still didn't understand what Kelly was driving at. Kelly noticed the bewildered look.

"It's simple really. All of the ducts come to this point eventually, it's like the heart of the place if you like. See those smaller ducts - tunnels almost like sewer drains?"

She pointed at the opening with the grid, the place where Alison had been looking.

"Well," she continued. "Jamie reckoned that these feed back into the main river, way over there. So the water was routed to here, then something to do with how the thing was built forced the water back through the ducts and eventually through the mill Wheel House."

"And it created more power or something?"

"Jamie's dad said that they reckoned it was a great idea - it enabled Martyn's Mille to have the power of three mills or more, all from a single water source."

"So Mr Smollett probably thinks we'll go exploring down drain holes and drown in the river!"

"I guess so," said Kelly. "Jamie's dad started to get nervous about us playing here too, when he found out. This was our secret, see. For a long time he didn't know we came here."

In one corner of the Quadrangle were the remains of steps, which jutted out from the side of the wall. She crossed to the corner and tried the first few.

"Be careful there," said Kelly. "Those things are crumbling."

Reaching out to steady herself, she slowly climbed, in places ascending two at a time. The steps finished just before the ridge at the top. Alison peered over the edge. Just behind her stretched the rest of the site, and on the far side was the wall which led through to the mill. A breeze blew up, which caught her off guard. A low whistle sounded across the tops of the ducts.

She looked back. A huge container - like the rear section of a truck, was parked nearby.

Beside this were more building materials, all of which were tied up, or covered in tarpaulins. She wondered what they were doing there, so far from the mill.

"You'd better come down," Kelly called. "It's really not too safe up there if you're not used to climbing."

Alison turned awkwardly and took a deep breath. Going down would be more difficult. But using juts of brick and stone in the wall to steady herself, she slowly descended.

About half way down she stopped for a moment and screwed up her eyes.

"What is it?" asked Kelly, who was watching her descent with some concern.

"It kind of looks different from here, the design or whatever it is on the floor looks magical."

Then one of the smaller ducts caught her attention. It was in the centre of the wall ahead. It had been almost invisible from the floor of the Quadrangle, but from here she could tell that there was a definite design. The rest of the surrounding cobble-stones and bricks seemed to point towards the centre, and the arch above the place had obviously been highly decorated with stone carvings at one time. Now they were crumbling and simply looked like battered statuettes.

With studied care she continued down to the floor of the Quadrangle. Kelly watched as Alison headed directly across the floor to the smaller duct. The opening had been sealed over with a dark coloured stone, but just above the floor near the centre was a hole. Beside the duct, in a small heap of brick dust and moss, were the remains of a chisel. The handle had cracked. Alison picked it up and looked closely at the end. Somebody had tried to chisel into the stone.

"A builder's been at this," said Alison.

Kelly stood a little way off. "That's what I thought. I overheard my uncle say something to one of the men last week. He had to make a test hole or something, to see if it was dry - like the others. I don't know why. He said he thought he'd found something in there. Uncle told him to just leave it."

Alison turned on her heels and looked up at Kelly. After a moment Kelly began to look away and grin.

"You sly boots," said Alison. "You found that whistle thing in there, didn't you?"

Kelly adjusted her cap then turned on her sharply.

"I was curious."

Alison turned back to the hole and lowered her head to listen. As with the other duct there was a distant echo, as of a far-off turmoil and rush. But this was different, somehow it sounded more turbulent, and she thought, almost angry.

She frowned, and turned her eye towards the opening, bending down to peer inside. Suddenly, she pulled away with a start.

Chapter 13

"I wonder. . ." began Sam Procter. He failed to finish his sentence, but remained seated on the pub chair. His son seemed equally thoughtful. Tim stood a little way off, watching the mountain form of Bob Walters scurry off into the crowd, holding carrier bags in each hand as if he were a pair of scales.

Sam felt in his jacket pocket for his phone, then looked for the scrap of paper on which he had written Bill Smollett's number at the mill.

For a few moments the mobile crackled and buzzed, and he had to shift around in his chair to pick up a connection. Then the ringing tone kicked in, and he was there. After a while a gruff sounding voice said, "Smollett."

"Bill," he said. "It's Sam Procter here. I'm still at the market. Look, I'm going to be later back than I expected."

Smollett sounded as if he were a voice in the air. "Nowt to worry about, we're getting on here."

"Bill, it's just that one of my kids is playing at the back - could you keep an eye? Remember, Alison - she's with Kelly - Geoff's niece. They're not your worry, of course - but just tell her I'll be back later this afternoon, perhaps earlier. There's bread and some bits and pieces in the kitchen. Tim's with me."

Smollett's voice seemed to rush into a storm,

echoed and bounced back again. "No problem Mr Procter - can you hear me?"

"Not too bad," said Sam. "Just before I go, there's something I need to ask you. Have you ever been approached, maybe two or three years ago, by a local chap called Dunn? To convert the mill?"

Sam thought he could hear the sound of Bill Smollett's breathing.

"Bill, can you hear me? Did you get that?"

An electrical buzz, like an angry wasp filled the phone. Sam shifted from his seat, turning to pick up a better signal.

"Bill," he repeated. "Did you get that? Do you know of a local man who was interested in the mill - name of Dunn?"

Sam cupped his hand over one ear and listened. Again, he thought he could hear Bill Smollett's breathing, as though he didn't know what to say. Then suddenly, he spoke.

"Mr Procter, I didn't catch that, this is a terrible line you know. Are you still there? The kids will be OK."

Suddenly the buzz returned and the phone went dead.

"Damn!" said Sam.

He slid the aerial down and switched off the phone. Tim had returned and was watching him.

"What are we doing, dad?" he asked.

Sam shook his head. "Nothing possibly - it was just an idea I had, but I don't think our

Mr Smollett wants to play."

Suddenly, he put his finger to his lips, as if struck by a sudden idea.

"The book stall, of course. Come on."

Almost galloping ahead of his son, Sam Procter began to weave his way through the thinning crowds. Many of the stalls were packing up for lunch, but a few who had produce to sell remained. Tim hurried behind him.

"I thought we might try and track this Mr Dunn and his family down, pay them a visit."

Tim called after him, "Why?"

"To find out if there's more to all of this than meets the eye - my hunch is that there is."

As they arrived at the book stall, two helpers were putting boxes in the back of a large van. Sam recognised one of the men who had served him.

"Hi," he said. "I was here earlier - got this book, in fact. I gather that this business was bought from a man called Dunn, perhaps a few years ago? Anyhow - to come to the point I'm trying to find him, can you help?"

"You've just missed the guvnor," said the man. "We're only casual - can't really help you."

"Your boss," Sam persisted. "Has he gone home? I mean could I call him, it is important?"

"Usually can," said the other man, who appeared with a box in his arms. "But not today - nor for the rest of the week. Him and his missus have gone off for a trip up the lakes."

"Thanks," said Sam.

Tim looked up at his father.

"How about the phone book?"

"Maybe we'll just have to forget it, for now. There's probably loads of Dunns. Come on, let's head back to the car - it was just an idea."

Slowly, they crossed to where they had parked the car. With a groan Sam Procter climbed in and tried to put on a brighter face. Tim stared ahead through the windscreen, then leaned forward in his seat. His father started the car.

"No," said Tim, pointing. "Not yet. Look - just in front of that shop."

Sam switched off the engine and looked in the direction of his son's finger. A young man in faded, grubby jeans and a T-shirt, leant against a signpost in front of a shop. Beside him was a brown leather carpet bag, which bulged with tools. A saw and a rule stuck out from one end.

"That's him," said Tim.

His father peered at the man. "Who? You mean that guy in the jeans."

"Yes," said Tim. "I'm pretty sure that was the workman in the white van, the night we arrived, the one that almost went into us."

Sam narrowed his eyes, "Are you sure? You might be right - but. . ."

"I saw his face, dad," said Tim, "and in any case, look at his bag - he's got to be a builder."

Sam opened the door. He hesitated, but decided to go up to the man. Tim jumped out and joined him.

"Hallo there," said Sam. "Excuse me for a moment, could you?"

The man was unsmiling. His mouth was downturned and he stared back at Sam with suspicion in his eyes.

"I don't think we've met before, but I believe you may have been working on my restaurant conversion - at Martyn's Mille? My name's Sam Procter."

The mention of the mill caught the man's attention more fully. He moved back for an instant. He had been playing with an old matchstick, and now placed this in the corner of his mouth, still saying nothing.

"We, my son and I, we thought that we recognised you."

After a minute, which seemed like eternity, he spoke. "I don't do 'owt there no more, got laid off by that damn bully."

Tim and his father exchanged looks.

"Oh, I see," said Sam. "That would be Mr Smollett?"

"Might be," he shifted the match to the other corner of his mouth.

"Look," said Sam. "I'm contracting Bill Smollett, and I'm worried about what's happening there - why we haven't got on as fast as I'd have liked with the work, that's all."

"We saw you drive past us the night that workman had his accident," said Tim. "You almost drove straight at us. It was you in the white van?"

Sam glared down at his son.

Suddenly, the man seemed to lose his hard attitude. He swallowed several times and gestured defensively with his hands.

"Now look, Mister, I'm sorry about that - there was no harm done. I just had to get away, couldn't stay there a moment longer."

"Why was that?" asked Sam. "We know about the so-called ghost, the serving girl. Did she make an appearance? Was that what happened, and you just got scared?"

The man's eyes moved restlessly in his head, and he broke out into a nervous giggle.

"Serving girl? Ha! You mean young Moll, as the story goes? Me, frightened of her!"
He took the match from his mouth and split it between his fingers.

"You didn't see her, then? OK what was it that made you drive off, and what made that other man - Ray somebody, wasn't it? - drop his drill?"

Tim noticed that beads of perspiration had broken out on the man's forehead. He began to glance to the side.

"I'm bound to keep my mouth shut. Smollett wants it that way. He gave me a pay-off. I knew I should never have gone there to work. It was just like before, the other time when I worked for old Boyce."

"Boyce?"

"Yeah, they were the other big firm here,

weren't they - gone bust now."

"You said something about the other time?" said Tim.

"It were a while ago. A couple were going to buy the place, I worked for old man Boyce. They were getting tenders in for the conversion work. I had to go there and suss it out like, for an estimate. Other builders put in bids too - but the project didn't go ahead."

Tim looked up at his father.

"Was it for some people called Dunn?" asked Sam.

The man grinned, but his eyes were still wild.

"Yeah. As a matter of fact. Yeah, it was Dunn."

"You won't tell us what happened?" said Sam, reaching for his wallet.

"No, no," he said. "I'm sorry, you'd think me crackers anyhow. But I live round here Mister and I want to go on working. Smollett's powerful. He paid me to keep my mouth shut, and for now that's what I'm going to do."

Sam kicked the ground with his heel. "Damn, it's like some huge terrible secret round here! How about if I was to find this Mr Dunn and asked him? That wouldn't land you in it, would it?"

The man suddenly rubbed his finger and thumb together. Sam Procter reached into his pocket and pulled out his wallet, and from that a banknote.

The fingers twitched again, and Sam pulled out a second.

The man snatched them, and with a wider, less nervous smile he reached into his bag. After a moment he pulled out a carpenter's pencil, and a scrap of paper. He scribbled an address and handed it to Sam.

"It ain't far from here. Village to the east - Warburton, just before you come into the village there's a farm road. He lives up there in a cottage, wi' his missus and that poor kid of his."

"Poor kid?" asked Tim.

"Just go and ask them about the place, they'll tell you. They'll put you right! There's more than our Miss Molly there now - believe me. Call me mad though - that's what they do - call me mad!"

He began to laugh.

Sam nodded and led his son back to the car. Once inside he let out a sigh of relief.

"What a character," he said.

Tim sat very still and watched the man's expression melt into one of dismay. For a moment he held his face in his hands.

"Something happened to him, didn't it, dad?"

"Right," said Sam ignoring his son's remark. "Let's see what we shall see. The Dunn's place it is."

Chapter 14

Alison balked for a moment and blinked rapidly. Her eyes stung and a thin trickle of tears ran down her cheek. She felt as though she had been briefly exposed to fumes of some kind, or something toxic. The hole in the stone shimmered, appearing to dilate. Vainly attempting to steady herself, she reached out and stumbled backwards.

Kelly had watched her, then realising she was in trouble, rushed forward to help.

"Are you OK? What was it?"

Alison pulled herself up straight against the wall and waited to compose herself. She couldn't answer Kelly's questions at first, and waited for tears to clear her vision. After a moment the stinging subsided.

"I don't know," she gasped. "It was like that stuff they put in hair products, what do you call it? - Ammonia. And there was something in there too, something crawling or scratching about. I heard it - I'm certain of it."

Within seconds Kelly was back at the stone, and very cautiously leaned forward to peer into the opening.

"Don't be stupid!" cried Alison. "There's gas or something like it being given off. Come away."

Kelly sniffed. "I'll be careful, I think there was a smell, but it's gone now. But you're right,

I can hear something too."

She leaned closer and spied into the opening, making certain that she kept some distance away. But she could see nothing at all. There was only darkness. Putting her finger in one ear to block out any surrounding sound, she lowered her other ear to the hole, and listened carefully.

"Can you hear anything?" asked Alison.

"Shush. Yes, I think I can."

All became still as Kelly strained to identify the far away undertones. After a few moments she stood back.

"There's this rushing noise, like wind or probably water - but that might be the river. Remember that all of these ducts are channelled through to the river system. But there's something else in there, a noise like somebody banging."

Alison joined her, and crouched beside the hole once again. Far off, as if in a secret place, she heard voices - whispers which sounded as if they were low murmured exchanges.

She pulled her head away.

"I don't hear banging, but there's two voices, or more." She listened again. "I don't believe it - I know this sounds ridiculous, but I think there's a conversation going on."

Kelly pulled Alison back and listened. After a second she jerked her head away suddenly, and stared back at the hole.

"What is it now?" asked Alison.

"You're right, there were voices, and I think I know why. Hang on a minute."

Kelly ran across to the steps, emptied her pockets of anything that might fall out, then like an agile and experienced climber, scaled the side of the wall.

Suddenly, Alison heard something rustle and scratch behind her. She turned back to face the opening in the stone.

She narrowed her eyes and cocked her head to one side. The opening in the stone looked different somehow, and a hair line crack had begun to spread, like a river tributary from one of the corners.

"It's got bigger," she whispered. "Heck - I'm certain."

She reached out and put her fingers just within the opening, and scraped. She felt something wet, like slime. For some reason she pulled her hand away quickly. The end of her middle finger was covered in a black tar-like substance. Slowly, she lifted it to her nose, and detected the ammonia smell again. She held her finger up to her face, and the tar began to trickle. For a second she thought that the stuff was beginning to burn. She quickly pulled a hanky from her shorts pocket and wiped her finger clean, with a cry of disgust. Then, as if it were something distasteful, she threw the hanky on to the floor.

"There's this horrible gooey stuff, Kelly," she said. "And unless I'm imagining things - this hole seems to have grown."

There was no reply.

"Kelly?" she called again, as she swivelled on her feet to look behind her. Kelly had reached the top and had gone.

"Kelly!" she cried, a note of panic creeping into her voice.

"It's alright - I'll be back in a second!" came a cry from somewhere above.

"Don't be long," yelled Alison. "I'm not crazy about being here."

A shiver shot down her spine.

Alison immediately felt uncomfortable at having been left alone. She wondered whether this might be what a wild animal felt like, when trapped in a pit. If only she could see above the rim, that would help. The sun had disappeared behind a thick cluster of cloud, and now a grey veil was slowly drawing across the sky.

A stirring of the breeze rustled the moss and wild flowers that hung at the edges of the Quadrangle. Away in the distance, she imagined voices calling her name.

"Hurry up, Kelly," she said, her teeth gritted tight.

Shapes weaved patterns across the floor.

"*Alison,*" came a voice.

Startled, she twisted round and stared at the stone.

"You're hearing things," she said aloud.

The breeze blew again, and this time a bunch of flowers blew into the Quadrangle and onto the floor. She crouched down and looked at them.

They were wild, and seemed common enough, like daisies or a similar weed, but there was something about them, something very different. They were turning black.

She blinked, and nervously reached out to pick them up. Slowly and carefully she twisted the stems between her fingers, turning them around so that she could inspect the petals. It was as if someone had dyed the edges, or dipped them in ink.

"*Alison*," came the cry again, her name carried through the ducts by the breeze.

She spun round and dropped the flowers.

A peculiar notion occurred to her: had the voice come from the hole in the stone?

"Occupy yourself," she said as she clenched her fists. She walked across to the steps and picked at Kelly's things which she had left there. There was a bunch of keys, some coins, and the whistle.

The whistle.

"*Alison*," came the voice again.

Suddenly, the name of their game flashed into her head: '*if you don't come to me, I will come to you.*'

She bent down and picked up the whistle. The inscription glistened - *Ye Summoner.*

'*If you don't come to me, I will come to you.*'

"Alison," repeated the voice.

This time it was unmistakable. Her name

had been called from the duct to her right. But it had been semi-sung this time, almost as though it had been a taunting, child-like voice. It was beckoning, she was certain of it.

Alison swallowed, gulping at air like a landed fish.

"Kelly? Kelly!"

Then she heard the sound of something snapping, crunching and cracking - like knuckles. Bone to the bone.

"Tim?" she immediately thought of him and his awful knuckle crunching habit. Had they returned?

"Tim - don't scare me."

'If you don't come to me, I will come to you.'

Almost without her realising it, she raised the whistle towards her face. Her eyes looked straight ahead, and step by step she turned towards the right hand duct.

It was like a slow march, one foot in front of the other, she walked as she lifted the whistle to her lips.

A tiny whisper of fine silvery mist blew from the hole in the stone. She never saw it.

'If you don't come to me, I will come to you.'

She walked on. Alison now found herself standing in the passage of the duct. The earth beneath her stirred like the soft sands of a desert. As she lifted one of her feet she became only slightly aware of a wetness. She stood quite, quite still. Snake-thin fingers reached up from the ground and searched for her ankle.

Nails gently scratched at her skin.

'If you don't come to me, I will come to you.'

Ahead, in the passage, like a floating filmy piece of silk cloth, came the shape. As it floated closer the face was too awful to imagine. Within the folds and clusters of the cloth was the face of the young girl, with that terrible grimace. After a second she became clearer, and Alison could see the serving maid's dress.

'If you don't come to me, I will come to you.'

The name of the game was like a tattoo in her head. Why wouldn't it leave? The image of Kelly flashed in front of her, of her standing in the duct earlier, with the whistle in front of her face. But that look - why hadn't she noticed it, the grin - the mischief, it had been a face that didn't belong to Kelly.

"Now you try too," said Kelly's image. "It's only a game."

Softly, and so, so slowly, Alison let her breath out of her body, past lips that barely touched, and into the end of the whistle.

"No! No! No!" came the scream.

It was a terrible rent, an anguished cry of a soul which ripped through the air like an arrow.

The face turned downwards and the shape descended into the earth.

Chapter 15

"Look out!" cried Tim.

Ahead of them, from out of nowhere, stepped the figure. The first thing that he saw was the staff - held out in front as though it were some kind of grotesque signal, then the fingers - long and pointed like claws.

Finally, the brown - there was the terrible haunting brown.

The coat or cloak, hung like a grave shroud on a frame thinner than seemed possible. Within the cowl was a grey flecked structure. The face was about to turn as the car was about to hit. Tim crouched down in his seat and screwed up his eyes.

"Dad!" he cried. "I don't want to see!"

"What, what is it?" yelled Sam Procter, who could only glance at his son for a second, before swerving the car to the side, and just avoiding a ditch in the road side.

Tim threw up his hands.

Had they passed right through it?

Then a split second later - it came; like a dark wave out of a cobalt blue.

The bird, a big black crow, hit the windscreen with the slap of a wet mass. The scream of the bird had been terrible. A death rattle, like the shriek of a burning banshee.

Sam put on his brakes and the car pulled to a halt with a forward shudder.

A red wash, with speckles of black feathers remained on the screen. Sam leant forward on the wheel and gasped.

He turned to Tim, who sat pale-faced and silent beside him.

"Are. . . are you alright?" he could barely manage the words.

Tim edged forward in his seat and timidly tried to see through the mess that coated the windscreen. The way ahead was clear, only the afternoon sky had begun to soften, as though preparing for the violet of the evening.

"Tim?" said his father once more.

Tim looked over his shoulder, anxious eyes searched for any sign of a dark hooded figure in brown. There was nobody there.

"Did we hit it?" he asked.

"I should say we did," said Sam. "How did you know though, it just dropped down from nowhere."

"I mean - the, the figure."

Sam unclipped his seat belt and got out of the car. Tim was quick to follow. He stared back down the road, which was a lonely series of curves that had stretched through fields for the past few miles since leaving Lofton. There was nothing to be seen - it was clear and easy to see for some way.

"I don't know what you're talking about, Tim," he said. "I think you just mistook the bird for something. It was quite a fright and. . ."

His words trailed off. Tim stood staring at

the windscreen of the car. His fingers barely touched his lips, but his eyes were wide with horror. The remains of the crow had begun to change. Instead of feathers and pulped flesh, the mess had begun to take on a life of its own. Slowly at first, the dark expanse of the wings shifted and crawled down from the screen. The sheen of the feathers lost their ability to catch the edges of light and became darker. Within moments the whole shape no longer resembled even the remains of a bird. Instead there was a black outline which crawled and dripped down on to the hood of the car.

As though transfixed by the stare of a snake, Sam stepped slowly forward.

"Move away, Tim," he said.

"What is it?"

"I've never seen anything like this before. Just move back."

Tim did as his father asked. Sam Procter meanwhile, reached in through the window for his keys and stepped round to the back of the car.

He unlocked the trunk, and hunted about. Then he seized a container of anti-freeze. He kept checking the front to see that his son was alright. Tim had stepped well back now. Within seconds Sam returned to the front. All that remained of the crow was a black shape which seemed to be thinning, like diluted ink. Holding the container out in front of him he vigorously shook the anti-freeze over the remains. For a second there seemed to be a reaction, then, as a shadow is dissolved by the rays of the sun, the inky remains streaked away from the screen and down the sides of the car.

He emptied the remains of the liquid until there was little or nothing left of the thing. Then he turned and looked at Tim. He was standing a little way back, cracking his knuckles without looking at his hands - it was almost an automatic reaction.

His son's face held a question which he did not ask. Sam felt helpless, useless, he had no answers.

"I just don't know," said Sam. "Come on, let's go."

The Dunn's cottage was set far back from the road, in a garden surrounded by firs and willows. On the gate had been a warning notice that stated *"No Callers - Hawksmen or Traders."* Sam and his son had said very little to one another as they had driven the further few miles.

As they walked up the path, Tim thought he saw a curtain shift in an upstairs window. He nudged his father who raised his finger to signal that he should remain silent.

The cottage was like most in the area - of cobblestone and flint, but there was a wild aspect to this setting. Ivy twisted in braids with russian vine to form a system of drapes. They fell from the roof and climbed the walls as though they had intended to be curtains, shutting out the world outside. Before they had even reached the door, Sam Procter sensed that the Dunns had become reclusive.

There was an old bell-pull outside the door, which was linked by a rusty chain to the bell spring. It jangled like a shop bell. Pinned on the door by a plastic headed tack was another warning to tradesmen.

They waited in silence. Sam thought he heard some scuffling inside the cottage. Tim stepped back and looked up at the window where he had seen the curtain move. For just a moment he thought he saw someone at the window; it was a boy's face, pale and empty, and he had looked down at him.

"There is somebody in," whispered Tim.

"I think so," said his father, again signalling for him to be quiet.

The sound of a chain sliding to one side, and the clunk of a turned lock, made both of them stand straighter. The door opened slightly, and a woman's face peered through the chink in the door.

"Yes?"

"It is Mrs Dunn?" said Sam.

"Who wants to know?" she said.

Behind her leaked the hiss of whispered voices, urgent and insistent. For a second she glanced back into the room.

"My name is Sam Procter," he said. "This is

my son Tim. Look, I'm sorry to just happen on you like this, but it's fairly important. I understand, if you are Mrs Dunn, that you and your husband were going to buy Martyn's Mille some while ago?"

The woman's face melted from that of cautious enquiry, to something else. Sam wasn't sure what, but there was a tinge of anxiety there, he was certain of it, and it was almost a fear of being asked anything else.

"Go away, we are private people - didn't you see the sign?"

"A moment, please," he reached out and put his hand against the door. "*Please*. I've some questions. You don't understand, I've bought the mill. I'm the new owner and there are some things that need explaining."

Her face changed again. It was almost as though she looked sorry for him.

"You've bought that place? I had heard something, my husband had too - something about a restaurant?"

Sam tried to smile. "That's right and we wanted to know why. . ."

He was cut short by a cry of realisation. The door was yanked back further, stretched wide on the chain. A small boy's face peered through the opening, past Sam and directly at Tim.

"You've seen, haven't you? *You know?*"

Tim Procter's jaw went slack. The boy's face was even paler than it had seemed at the upstairs window. But the whites of his eyes betrayed a glint of madness, and recognition, as though in Tim he had found the other half of himself.

Chapter 16

Kelly slowly stepped forward and pushed her face into Alison's. Alison was in another place, awake and yet somewhere dark and empty.

Kelly shook her - gently at first, without any reaction, then she lifted her hand and slapped her hard around the face. Alison snapped back with a sharp intake of breath.

"What happened?" Kelly asked. "You were just standing there, it was weird."

Alison appeared dazed.

"I don't know," she said. "But I saw her, I'm certain of it - I saw Molly Gates. I don't know if it was a vision, a dream or what - but I saw her again."

Alison's face took on a stern and serious expression. "Look Kelly - she's afraid. There's something here, or there *was* something here, that terrifies her! Can you understand that? We've a ghost that is afraid, her scream is terrible. I think that every time we see her, she is re-enacting the event that made her fall. What was it she said? *'Now it's dark'* - it was a hopeless thing to say."

She gasped and struggled to hold back her tears. "What was it she saw, Kelly, what was it that scared her so much?"

"Come on, you'll be OK," said Kelly. "I was right about the voices though. I've just checked above. The duct leads through to the bottom of the Wheel House. Those were workmen's voices - I thought so, but I needed to make sure. I called out to you, didn't you hear me? It was a test."

Alison gaped. A sudden rush of release sped through her.

"That was you? What did you call, what did you call out?"

"Your name, I called out Alison. Hey, calm down."

"I thought I was dreaming, imagining things or something. Was there anything else?"

"I may have called out the Mother Gudgeon thing or something. Some new workmen were taking a look at the site. They were discussing what they had to do there with Mr Smollett and my uncle. Uncle said that the duct did lead back to the mill, it links with the river too."

Alison's face showed relief. She brushed back her hair and rubbed away a tear with her hand.

"We've been asked to go back to the mill by Mr Smollett. Your dad's going to be back late - he called Mr Smollett, and now they've all gone off to collect some equipment or other stuff. They've left one of the workmen here to keep an eye on things, he asked if we can help."

"I think I've had enough down here," said Alison dryly.

"Oh, by the way," said Kelly. "Let me show you something."

She went to the black stone and stooped on

her haunches. For a moment it was clear that she wasn't certain what she was looking for. She peered closely at the edges of the stone and then clucked her tongue.

"Got it, come and see."

Alison crouched down beside her.

"Uncle said that they had to make the hole to test it for something. But there was this big iron door in front of it, look in the crack here at the side - you can see where the hinges had been prised out. Mr Smollett said it was really difficult to get off - thought it was better than a bank safe!"

Kelly laughed.

Alison didn't.

Instead she had turned her attention to another part of the stone. The crack had grown, and now was making its way downward to the base.

"It's going to break," said Alison. "And look at the hole, is it bigger?"

Kelly wrinkled her nose.

"Maybe it's just breaking up because it's been weakened?"

That seemed to make sense to Alison.

"Come on," said Kelly. "I told this workman we'd help him with putting in some light bulbs - and it's a real neat door, I've got to show it you. My uncle was going to clean it up and present it to your dad. He thought it would look great in the restaurant."

Alison looked upwards. The late afternoon

seemed to be drawing in faster than was usual. The light was decaying.

Back at the mill, Allan Fisher, the new workman on Smollett's team was cheerfully stacking boxes of light bulbs in the passage. He looked up as he saw Kelly and Alison cross the bridge towards him.

"Hey!" he called.

"This is Alison," said Kelly. "Her dad owns the mill. You said you wanted some help?"

"Hi, Alison," he said. "OK then. Don't go climbing any high steps, though, we don't want any more accidents by the sound of things. We're having another go at lighting up the place. Must say I've not seen anything like it before."

"What's wrong?" asked Alison.

"I think my uncle mentioned it to your dad," said Kelly. "They can't seem to light the place properly."

"And it seems to be getting worse," said Fisher. "Earlier on today a whole bank of lights blew. It's kind of dark in some parts of the mill and the men can't see clearly enough what they're doing. Bulbs just blow, even candles in the Wheel House snuffed out from sudden gusts of air. This place doesn't like light."

Suddenly, he seemed less cheerful. He put down a box and held his shoulders.

"It's an odd site, is this."

Alison watched him. He seemed suddenly vulnerable, unhappy at being on his own there, with just two kids for company.

"I'm not getting spooked, though," he said. "One of the other lads has tried to do that already. Come on kids, it looks a touch like rain. Let's get inside. The light bulbs - seek out and plug in!"

Alison and Kelly worked their way through the rooms from the front of the mill. The builder said that he would do the trickier places in the rear of the building.

There was broken glass almost everywhere. Most of the remains of the bulbs had been removed from the sockets, but in some the bare filament was still stuck in the holder. Although Fisher had told them to leave these to him, Kelly managed using a rag to protect her hand.

"They shouldn't just blow up, surely?" said Alison, after they had fitted a dozen new bulbs.

Kelly shrugged her shoulders. "I don't know. I did hear my uncle talking to my dad once about it. It was when they first started here, even lights from their generator went out."

"This place doesn't like light."

Fisher's remark echoed once again in Alison's head.

Finally, they fixed the lights in one of the

rear rooms to the left of the passage. Although it was only late afternoon, the shadows which the bulbs threw seemed somehow larger than was usual. This notion occupied Alison for some while, and she repeatedly entered the room and compared the way the light fell there, to the gloom of the passageway outside.

"I think this is going to be a supplies room," said Kelly. "I heard them say so."

Alison stood opposite, watching her shadow move, and looking into the corners of the room. They had fitted two low-powered bulbs here, in wall sockets near the door.

She crossed to the opposite corner, and surveyed her surroundings once again. Then she stared up at the ceiling. There was only one small window opposite, which looked out onto another view of the Wheel House.

Kelly watched her, waiting for her to explain what it was that she was doing.

"Kelly," Alison said after a moment. "Do there seem to be more shadows in here than there are people, or things to be able to throw shapes - do you follow me?"

At first Kelly wasn't sure what she meant. Then she put her own arm out in front of her. A multiple of shadow shapes spread across the floor.

"Hey, you're right."

She looked up at the two lights for a moment, then stood beneath one of them, which was closest to the door.

"Nah," she said. "It's the effect of the bulbs - look."

"Turn them off for a moment," said Alison.

Slowly, Kelly reached up and switched out the light.

Chapter 17

The intensity of the light inside the cottage startled Sam and Tim. Not only were all the house lights switched on, but extra lights had been brought into the lounge: there were desk lamps and standard lamps, and in the corners were floodlights - but these were switched off.

The second thing that startled them was the atmosphere. Bare beams divided the main lounge from another area, which stretched through to the back of the place. Here, in a far corner, sat Mr Dunn - sombre-faced in an easy chair. Mrs Dunn looked haunted, and she carried herself with a nervous disposition. But the boy - Jamie Dunn, just sat on a stool near the brightest of the desk lamps, rocking gently backwards and forwards as though in an obsessive state of trance.

Mrs Dunn had hurriedly made tea and had brought them a cup each. Jamie had said nothing further, and Mr Dunn had simply nodded out of politeness.

Sam tried desperately to accept that this was a family who once had thought themselves to be entrepreneurs; and that they had seriously considered buying his mill. They just didn't look the type.

After an awkward gap, during which Sam and Tim simply gazed in wonder around them, Mrs Dunn finally spoke up.

"You may have heard of our Jamie's little problem," she said, nodding in the boy's direction.

"Er, no," said Sam, caught unawares. "No - not at all. I think one or two people alluded to something or other. I think they just said something innocent like - poor kid."

Again the boy stared at Tim, his rocking became faster.

"You've seen. You know, don't you?" he said.

"Know what, seen what?" said Tim, softly. His father coughed.

"Don't upset yourself," said Mrs Dunn, smiling benevolently at her son. She made a deep sigh and pulled herself up straight.

"It's fear of the dark," said a voice from the corner room. It was Mr Dunn. He had been sucking on an old briar pipe.

"I'm sorry?" said Sam.

"His condition, the lad's problem. It's fear of the dark. Come on, Mr Procter, don't tell me you haven't noticed that we're lit up like a bloomin' sports stadium here."

"No," smiled Sam, trying to be as gentle as he could. "Of course, I noticed."

"He were worse today," said Mrs Dunn. "And he had a sudden outburst about half an hour ago. That was why I'm so edgy."

"Half an hour ago?" repeated Tim. He checked his watch, and for a second he thought back to the incident on the road - that was half an hour ago.

"We don't always have them on," said Mrs Dunn. "Just his phases. But there are times when he's so bad that we have to sit here with him with dark glasses. It were much worse earlier in the beginning. He's better now."

Sam tried to gather his thoughts, puzzling over how to approach his questions. But the Dunns were starting to open up, to become more chatty.

"The GP called it something fancy," said Mr Dunn. "Obsessional behaviour, sparked off by something. He'll grow out of it though."

Tim watched the boy rocking on his stool; the stark eyes in his otherwise empty face were fixed on his own.

"*Obsessional behaviour!*" snapped Mrs Dunn. "Both you and I know better, you know we do!"

"Keep counsel!" said Mr Dunn, pulling his pipe from his mouth. "Company!"

The silence was thick and full. Only the creaking of Jamie's stool cut into the iciness of the moment.

"What can we do for you, Mr Procter?" sighed Mr Dunn. He rose from his chair and stepped into the sitting room. For a moment he stopped by his son, and squeezed his shoulder reassuringly.

Sam Procter cleared his throat. "I'm having a few problems - it's the workmen. They seem reluctant to work there. There's supposed to be this serving girl ghost. I thought that one of the builders might have seen it - he had an accident, in the dark. He saw something. So did his work mate, I think you know him, John Cooper. He was involved in a survey for you once. He won't talk. He said that I should ask you about the place."

Mr and Mrs Dunn looked at each other. Mrs Dunn gestured at Jamie.

"Won't matter," said Mr Dunn. "He's happy rocking, just rocking and laughing - rocking and laughing. Boy's elsewhere."

He placed his pipe on the mantelpiece and turned to Sam.

"You said they were frightened by something? It was the serving girl, of course?"

Sam's face became stone. "I think they'd like to make me believe that." He looked over at Tim, then at Jamie. He was rocking still, his eyes still empty since his outburst. "I think there's something else. We can't light the place."

Mrs Dunn swallowed a gasp. Mr Dunn glared at his wife.

"You've got kids, clearly Mr Procter," she said quietly.

"Tim here, and a girl - Alison, she's back at the mill playing with a friend, foreman's daughter - Kelly."

"Oh God!" said Mrs Dunn.

Sam sat up; Tim caught his breath.

"Quiet, woman!" said Mr Dunn.

"No, no John," she said. "We've got to tell

him. If he thinks we're mad, it's for him to decide."

"Tell me what, Mrs Dunn?" This time Sam was more determined. A sliver of unease which had been pricking away at him, had now become a wedge. He fidgeted in his chair. The creaking of the stool was starting to grate on his nerves.

"Do you believe in evil, Mr Procter?" said Mrs Dunn.

Mr Dunn stepped near his wife. He reached out to touch her, then pulled his hand back. She looked up at him with sad eyes.

"Yes," said Sam. "I believe I do."

"And what about that which we call the unknown - the supernatural. Do you believe in ghosts?"

He hesitated. "I've never seen one. Though since coming here it seems that there's plenty that do. I've heard about Molly Gates, of course."

"And you know that she was found with this terrible look about her?"

He nodded.

"What do you think put it there, Mr Procter? She was scared to death. When me and him were going to buy the place, we spent time there looking round, planning and the like. It started off by us having picnics in the woods - Martyn's Place. We had no idea that Jamie was playing in the mill grounds. He were friends with Bob Walters' girl. She was a nice lass, but together they explored more than they should. Weren't her fault, but you know how kids lead one another on."

She looked across at Jamie. Then her eyes flicked back to Sam. Now they were intense.

"John had his book stall, and was well in on local history. We found these piles of papers in between the leaves of an old ledger. I'll give you a short version because between us we pieced it all together from all kinds of stories. Martyn's Place is older than you might think. Goes back to Saxon times. Charcoal burners used the place. There were talk of dark practices there, that it was somehow a magical place for black art ceremonies. Part of it were a small holding too, a farm. It was farmed and minded by a 'crone' - a Weird. Stories tell that she had familiars and would do harm to any soul if she were paid enough. Some came from hundreds of miles to buy her magic - she was powerful. A circuit Judge called her the blackest witch ever recorded in these parts. The place was bought up by a Squire - Martyn Medlock. He gave notice to the crone - Old Mother Gudgeon were her name. He wanted to build the mill, see. And a grand house. He certainly didn't want any truck with Gudgeon."

"Well, she didn't want to leave, did our Old Mother Gudgeon. She swore that nothing would ever be built there, that she would set a guardian over the place. Medlock ignored her and built the first mill, with those aqueducts.

She still had her place, to the side in the woods. She said that no light would ever shine there, that it would be an eternal tomb of darkness. One day she mysteriously vanished."

"They found her, of course," said Mr Dunn. "Her throat was cut, little doubt that she had been murdered. The men that did it were found with plague a month later."

"Then it was just a trail of disaster," said Mrs Dunn. "They couldn't manage candle-light there, and that was why the fire broke out. There were others - a new mill was built, but it just couldn't survive. There was always something. I believe our Molly Gates glimpsed Old Mother Gudgeon's guardian, and she fell down the steps to her death."

"Or maybe that which was guarded. We don't know. Fear of the dark," said Mr Dunn. "Call us mad if you like, but nobody's touched that damned place. It's cursed and we wanted none of it."

Mr Dunn bit his bottom lip. "The tale gets blacker," he said.

"Then, *he* saw something," said Mrs Dunn. She crossed the room and kissed the top of her son's head. "We heard of a Summoner - references in old ledger diaries - we couldn't fathom out what that was for a while. But there were two keys to this terrible darkness. Jamie found one in the ruins at the back in that Quadrangle thing. It was something like a flute, carved out of bone we thought, and there was an inscription. That's when we knew. Thank God - nobody found the second, but it was supposed to be down there too. We crushed the thing, and powdered it into dust. But he'd blown down it, his own sweet innocent breath - he'd summoned the Guardian, glimpsed it. We are just thankful that he or we, never got to discover what it was that it guarded."

A crack of silence entered the room. The creaking of the stool ceased. Sam Procter turned his face towards his son, but he was staring in horror at Jamie.

"A brown figure," hissed Tim. "Tell me. The Guardian? It's a wiry creature with a staff, and a face I never want to see? Isn't it?"

Jamie stood up, tears beginning to trail from his eyes. He reached out towards a nearby lamp and stared into the ray of the light.

"*You know*. I told you, it's been summoned. You must realise - *it's been summoned!*"

Chapter 18

The immediacy of the sudden darkness made Alison shudder. She had not been expecting that the room would be plunged into quite such a chasm of blackness. A muted glow came from somewhere out in the hall. Outside the window, the light had turned to a violet sheen. The edges of stone shone as if imbued with a magical quality, but across the scene, like a thinly pasted gauze, was a presence unlike anything Alison had seen before.

"It swallows light," she whispered. "The very air here just eats it. It's like a struggle between light and dark."

"The darkness is coming," said Kelly. Her voice sounded strange, it was as though she had mouthed words which were not her own.

Suddenly, from outside the window came a tapping. But there was nobody there.

"The Mother's brood," said Kelly in words barely spoken.

The tapping returned - more urgent than before.

Alison looked again, and floating in space, peering in at them, was the form of Molly Gates. Alison cried out, a tiny cry which stuck at the back of her throat. She stared at the thing which hung there - a face as before, stuck forever in an expression of terror.

Alison crossed to the window and pressed

her hand against the glass. On the other side of the window, the girl was tap-tap tapping with her nails on the pane.

"What, what is it?" said Kelly. For a second she regained her own voice.

"You can't see her, can you?" said Alison. She looked into the face behind the window. The girl's mouth did not make any words, but inside her head she heard a voice, as clear as ringing crystal.

"Now it's dark, sweet Lord save me, it's so, so dark."

This time Alison felt less afraid. It was as though an old friend had visited her. The warning came again. *"Be wary. Be aware."*

"Of what?" said Alison. "Of what must we be aware?"

Her response echoed at the back of her head. *"Of the dark, it's been let out. Look to the flowers to know, look to the flowers."*

The rap of her nails faded away and was replaced by the gentle patter of rain.

The girl glimmered like an incandescent glow. Then, as if washed away by the rain, she rippled and broke into wispy strands.

Kelly switched on the light. For a moment it was as though someone had turned on the sun. Her face was turned towards the window, and she looked hot and angry.

"Flowers," Alison said, half to herself as if repeating an instruction. "She said I was to look to the flowers. Come on, I need to know what she means."

There was nobody in the passage, but looking past the end door, which Allan Fisher the builder had left open, they saw a shifting light from the Wheel House.

"He's still out back," said Alison.

She briskly walked down the passageway to the bridge. Kelly drifted behind as though suddenly dazed. Just as they reached the door, Alison stopped. She had stubbed her foot against something that leant against the wall. In the gloom it seemed like a stone slab, then she reached out and felt the edge. It was metal, and it felt smooth and polished.

"Hang on," she said. "They've put that door here, the thing that was in the Quadrangle. I've got a feeling about this, I must look at it."

She tried to move it into the light but it was too heavy.

"I've a torch in my room," said Alison.
She ran to the bedroom, and within moments re-appeared with a heavy-duty torch. She flashed the light at the door.

"They've blasted it, or cleaned it with something special," she said as she passed the torch to Kelly. "Hold it, hold the light there."

In the centre of the plate was a series of loops and whorls, above which was a name.

She peered closer. For a brief moment the torch beam faded and then became brighter again.

"Batteries?" asked Kelly.

"I don't think so," said Alison.

Now she could see the name.

"It says - CUSTODIAN. And there's something in smaller writing below: *Forever more, a Guardian has been set to watch over this place.*"

She looked closer at the border.

"There's figures here, etched in the metal, and they look as if they are being swallowed up or drowned in this wave thing."

Kelly watched as Alison traced her finger around the edge of the door. A ribbon seemed to be following the figures; in places it entwined them. It would have been innocent enough except that the little figures seemed to be in varying states of anguish. The detail was alarming.

Suddenly, the hand torch failed.

"Come on," said Alison. "Let's see outside - you know, about the flowers and things."

They stood at the far end of the bridge. It was evening by now, and there was no sign of anybody having returned. The halogen lamps on the poles had switched themselves on. By now the sky had become a deep grey wash.

"Do you notice the light, Kelly?" she said. "I've never seen anything like it, what's happening here?"

Kelly suddenly pointed into a cluster of shrubs and weeds. They ran to the spot.

"What is it?" said Alison. "I saw something like this in the aqueducts. Look at the leaves -

look at the flowers."

Kelly reached out to pick a bunch. Alison shot out her hand and held her wrist. "No!" she said.

The green leaves had turned to black. The petals were also affected, and as they stood there, they gradually realised that the same effect was creeping through the rest of the ground, through the grass and beyond.

"This can't be," said Alison. Slowly, in uncomprehending gasps of disbelief, she walked towards the trees. The colour of the edges of the leaves were just picked out by the rays of the halogen. They were sooty black. And as she traced these back along the branches, and into the trunk, she realised that the place was changing colour. As though suddenly imbued with an evil stain, Martyn's Place was changing into a mark of darkness, the colour being drained.

"A Guardian has been set to watch over this place," whispered Kelly.

She pointed at the sky. The form of a rising silver moon had appeared low in the horizon. It was a hungry disc which sparkled like dead fish scales. The shimmering aura struggled with wisps of dark cloud. And from the other side, from the face which is never seen, seeped a fine vein of black fissures. They weaved into the sky like seeking fingers.

From the Wheel House came the scream of Allan Fisher. It echoed into the trees and scared the birds.

Kelly turned and smiled, almost with a look of triumph.

Chapter 19

They stepped out into the garden. Jamie remained inside, shivering nervously. His anxious eyes were rolling like mad marbles now. Mrs Dunn stood in the doorway, looked up and muttered, 'Help us all', then hurried back inside to comfort her son.

Sam Procter checked his watch - it was only five o'clock. Yet in the heavens the sun was fading. The moon was asserting itself like an invading body, its face a craggy scape. But it was the sky itself that alarmed them. A net was being thrown across their world.

Sam tried his mobile to call the mill. But it was impossible to become connected. The receiver buzzed angrily, as if the air waves were full of dark voices - hissing and spitefully spitting into their invaded space.

Tim stood in the centre of the lawn. He raised his hand to his forehead and tried to see. At the far end of the garden, pines swayed with the force of the gathering wind. It was there - within the trees, but it stood defiantly, no longer a glimpsed spectre.

Tim Procter walked across the lawn and stood a little way from the boundary. The ragged brown flapped as though it were a scarecrow on a windy night. The figure moved forward, hovering silently and perfectly above the ground; spindly legs, which did not take steps, trailed backwards.

"I don't want to see the face, please don't let me see the face," the thought pierced Tim's mind like a needle. But he could not look away. He walked forward.

The figure's head was bowed, and the cowl drooped loosely around its head like a hood. The staff which it bore like a shepherd's crook, was held ahead. It floated closer.

Tim stepped forward.

Suddenly, a gale blew up. It shook the bushes and the trees with an angry lash. The path that led to the cottage rippled. The gravel rose and fell like a gentle pulse. From nowhere, stones spat into the air; somewhere else a crack of lightning split the sky.

Tim's eyes grew wild and wide.

The figure lifted its head. For a moment he glimpsed the bone and the crusted jaw line. A hand with fingers like claws reached towards the cowl, and pulled it back from its face.

Tim saw. A chasm of darkness yawned towards him.

From the cottage, Sam had watched his son step towards the end of the garden. Tim had seemed to be drawn by something, but he had not seen what.

Suddenly, from inside the house, Jamie shrieked. His mother pulled him closer to her. But he kept repeating, over and over - "It's here, it's here."

At almost the same moment, Sam saw his son fold like a collapsed chair.

"Tim!" he yelled, and sprinted across the garden to his son.

The voice of Mr Dunn tried to carry through the chaos.

"What's happened at the mill? It were fine till you came. Oh, my God, you've done summin, you've let it out!"

Chapter 20

At almost the precise moment they heard Allan Fisher's voice, the light bulbs inside the house grew like balloons and exploded. The darkness within the mill was sudden, but not complete. In the forecourt the halogen lamps flickered, one went out - but the other became steady again.

Alison grabbed Kelly's arm.

"The Wheel House," said Alison as she felt her whole body shudder. "It's in the Wheel House."

Kelly did not respond. Alison started for the bridge, then looked back. Beneath the glow of the halogen Kelly stood like a statue, the whistle held in front of her, inches from her lips.

Alison looked back across the bridge. From within the passageway which led to the rear came a form which stumbled from side to side. The doors swung wide, and the wild man figure of Allan Fisher flopped into the light.

He rushed across the bridge with arms that swung from side to side like an ape's.

"Hey, wait. . ." Alison began.

But he rushed past her, and she noticed that his mouth was yanked into a limp-lipped oval. He was making tiny cries, like those made by a small frightened child.

"Mr Fisher?" said Alison, her voice a cross

between bewilderment and fear.

She turned suddenly towards Kelly. The whistle was at her lips again. But it was her stance that chilled Alison. Her feet were apart, and the look on her face was determined and focused.

"Kelly, what's wrong with you?" she cried. "What's happening here?"

Beyond her, Fisher stumbled and fell to the ground. His cries were muffled gasps, which he mouthed into the earth. A slash of light lit up his body. There was something black, like heaped tar, clinging to his back. It writhed as if possessed with a life of its own.

Suddenly, the doors of the passage crashed open.

Alison saw it.

It moved with stealth, an animal stealth as though with intelligence. It was like a dark lava flow, and in flashes it seemed that the thing lifted itself - then shaped itself into tendril fingers which reached out and found another direction.

Against the crackle of the sky came the most awful final touch of all. It was Kelly's laughter.

Alison twisted round. Kelly looked strangely powerful. Then the rains came, and she held out her hands wide. She cried in a voice which rose above the thunder.

'If you don't come to me, I will come to you.'

Alison watched in silence, as with each second that passed Kelly seemed to become pitted with dark marks. Then she held out her own hands in front of her and cried out once more.

'Old Mother Gudgeon has got you!'

It was raining blackness: a liquid darkness which pitted the ground and the pot-hole puddles around her. It was as though a demonic ink had poured down on to them.

Suddenly, from somewhere in the trees, Alison thought she saw a pair of head lamps. Beams bounced off tree trunks as the over-revved roar of an engine came closer. Her heartbeat rose into her ears, blocking out the bedlam of noise.

"Dad, Tim, please let that be you, *please*!"

The slam of car doors reassured her. But the faces that beamed at her, glowing from the reflections of their torches, were not what she had hoped for.

But it was help.

Bill Smollett and Geoff Walters stood gaping at the scene, the shock momentarily freezing them to the spot. Alison's yell snapped them out of it. Smollett rushed over to his workman, who was clawing at the ground, picking lumps of muddy slime, and letting it squeeze through his fingers. Walters ran to his niece, who still stood in the rain, arms outstretched in a hideous welcome. The black rain had streaked down her face; she looked like a forest sprite, a demon in tribal paint.

"The whistle - the thing in her hand! Snap it,

can you break it?"

Walters wondered what she meant, then realised the madness in Kelly's eyes and saw the stubby tube which she held in her hand. He grabbed it, and with a second stamp under his heel, crushed the thing in two.

Kelly took a sharp intake of breath, then a look of recognition returned to her face.

"All hell has been released out there, we couldn't see where or what we were doing," said Smollett. "What on earth is going on?"

"It's the Prophecy, isn't it. It's the old legend come true," cried Walters. "I warned you. Meddling and messing! Who would ever have thought that. . ."

He broke down, as Kelly looked up with a pleading gaze of animal helplessness.

Suddenly, the bridge began to creak. From across the bank came the creeping evil, the product of Old Mother Gudgeon's curse - a shape that knew its task. Deep inside the ebony shadow, pin prick eyes were set within a folding horror of melting bone, blood and sinew which was tossed together like some devil's brew. There was a partially discernible face within the form, features which kept shifting and changing. Only now could Alison see it. It was ancient and menacing, a face of revenge, of an evil woman who had felt wronged hundreds of years previously, and had been buried beneath the mill.

"It's trying to reclaim the land," said Walters.

"It'll run through the whole of Lofton!"

And then the flow retreated. Tributaries, like tendrils - tubes of shadow, pulled back to the mother form. It withdrew from the bridge, and sloped back into the passage.

"I know where it's going!" Alison shouted. "Tell me again, what was it you said?"

Walters stuttered. "About Lofton? - I said it's trying to reclaim the land, to poison it."

"It's seeking out the aqueducts, that's the way, isn't it? That would be the way to reclaim the land?"

Bill Smollett had calmed Allan Fisher, and sat him against a tree. He crossed to the others. Kelly now hung on to her uncle, afraid and uncertain of what was going on.

"What is that thing?" he said.

"I don't know," said Alison, "but I think Kelly summoned it and you let it out. The duct with the door, I think it was somehow imprisoned there. It's making its way back into the Quadrangle. That's the heart of Martyn's Place, isn't it?"

"Yes, yes it is," said Smollett.

He grated his teeth, then his eyes flashed with an idea.

"It slithers, it moves like mud - like water?"

Alison's face grew into an excited oval. The rain came harder now.

"The Quadrangle - you were planning to - "

"Fill it in!" yelled Bill Smollett. "Fill the whole thing in and I've a container of dry mix standing by. Come on!"

Kelly stayed with Allan Fisher, after quick reassurance from her uncle. The three of them rushed around the side, not daring to follow the trail of the thing directly. Alison was in the lead, darting and finding her way from the instant daylight of lightning flashes.

At the back of the mill, the old site was already roaring with the rush of water from a gorged river, made worse from the rain mixing with the shape.

Sam Smollett ran along the southern boundary of the site towards the container, whilst Geoff Walters managed to gain speed and reach the container before him. He heaved on the wheel which directed the chute above the Lower Quadrangle.

For seconds night turned to brightest day, and he cried out. The thing below writhed and heaved like an angry sea. Never before had he seen folds of shadow, folds which made up a face that damned him with each dart of silver which shook the sky.

"Switch on, Geoff," said Smollett. He had connected the water to the load, the mix had little time left to be prepared.

A creak of gears, and the scraping of cogs and wheels accompanied the roar of the water into the container.

Alison stood at the edge of the Quadrangle. The shape appeared to have organised itself, and was beginning to enter the ducts that terminated here.

"We can't wait! Not any longer!" said Alison.

Smollett nodded, and Geoff Walters threw the lever which emptied the cement mix into the pit.

Almost immediately there was a thrashing below. Black waves slapped against the side of the Quadrangle as the grey of the mix weaved and entered the thing. At first it looked as though it was a swirl of coloured sands. Thousands of tiny grey rivers diluted the blackness and gradually, the thing's thrashing changed to a different consistency.

From somewhere deep in the heart of the earth came a cry, more awful than Alison had ever heard before.

Geoff Walters threw a second lever, the container tilted and a second load emptied on to the first.

Bubbles rose and almost before their eyes the quadrangle lifted and became gorged with a lake of dark grey.

A flash of light peeled back the sky as though it were the skin of some fruit.

Alison looked up.

The moon cracked and crazed like a plate, and the silvery skein ran into the fleeting dark clouds. The orange of a late setting sun broke through.

Walters grinned at Smollett.

"I put some rapid mix in, remember we argued over whether it was worth it?"

But Smollett did not smile, he stared and stared at the ripples, which struggled to make an outline as the stirring of the mixture slowed to a halt.

"Oh, no," said Alison, as she saw what he saw.

"That face," he whispered, unable to hide his revulsion.

"It's all alright," said Mrs Dunn. "It's all better again."

They suddenly became aware of the bird song, as the sudden storm - the sudden unnatural night, fled away to the far horizon.

Jamie appeared bright eyed, smiling. Mrs Dunn put her hand to her mouth, unable to speak.

"Something's cleared it, something's sorted it," said Mr Dunn.

Tim blinked and looked up at his father. He felt as if he had been in a trance, somewhere in another time.

Sam Procter tried to control his shaking hand as he reached for his mobile phone, and tried Martyn's Mill, and Bill Smollett, once more.

Epilogue

"Oh dear, my my now," said Jenny Procter. Sam Procter's wife had been collecting payment for the bill from a young couple, who had dined outside in the courtyard.

Their little girl had run to them in tears.

"What on earth's the matter?" said Jenny, bending down to wipe the child's tears with a handkerchief.

Behind her came Alison, who had been helping to clear the tables. It was late afternoon and they had to prepare for the next evening shift of Lofton's most successful restaurant.

"Mum, here a minute," she said.

Jenny stepped back to join her daughter.

"She was playing at the back, she was looking into the Quadrangle."

Jenny Procter sighed.

"She'll be alright," said the mother of the little girl. "She thought she saw something odd at the back there - she's got such an imagination!"

The little girl glanced up, almost angrily. "But I did see it, the face of a horrible lady! It was laughing at me - it was nasty!"

She burst into tears again.

Later that afternoon Jenny Procter stood with her daughter looking down at the Quadrangle.

"You've never believed us, have you?" said Alison. "Dad and Mr Smollett did a deal - that's why you never hear of anything."

Jenny Procter put her head to one side, and stared yet again, as she did almost every day. The strange shapes and curves in the otherwise smooth surface meant nothing to her. She sighed and walked away.

A chill ran through Alison Procter's bones. She could see it so clearly.

Too clearly.

Forever moulded into the concrete was the death mask of Old Mother Gudgeon. A wave of folded concrete made the nose, and another the terrible mouth. And there were the scooped hollows - the bowls making up the eyes. She could never stare at them for long.

Never.